Captain Teeth

A Monster Brides Romance

By Marilyn Barr

Walk the Walk

Book 5: Hooking Captain Teeth

Walk the Walk

Book 5: Hooking Captain Teeth

All rights reserved. No part of this publication may be reproduced, distributed, or transmitted in any form or by any means, including photocopying, recording, or other electronic or mechanical methods, without the prior written permission of the publisher, except in the case of brief quotations embodied in critical reviews and certain other noncommercial uses permitted by copyright law. For permission requests, write to the author, addressed "Attention: Permissions Coordinator," using the contact form on the website below.

Copyright © 2024 Marilyn Barr.

Any references to historical events, real people, or real places are used fictitiously. Names, characters, and places are products of the author's imagination. Made by humans.

Front cover image by Brylle Axeford of Cangxxx Graphics.

Edited by Evil Commas

Chapter Heading Tentacles Image by Cloud7Days via DepositPhotos

Ship Scene Break Image by Mogil via DepositPhotos

Printed in the United States of America.

First printing edition 2024.

www.marilynbarr.com/

Walk the Walk

Book 5: Hooking Captain Teeth

Walk the Walk

Book 5: Hooking Captain Teeth

Dedication

To the readers who fell in love with Teeth four books ago and clamored for his book. We've been waiting for his match to appear and she's worth the wait.

Content Warning

This book is for adults with bloody, pirate violence, and steamy romantic scenes between a consenting human and a monster shifter. Their steamy scenes include tentacle play which leaves no holes untouched. Teeth's voyage to Sabrina's heart involves sex work positivity, kidnapping, sexual assault (by the villain, not by our swashbucklers), and exploitation of others in an old-timey sideshow. And while me hearties rescue all the show's participants, opening their pirate ship as a place to heal from their exploitation, please read with caution.

Walk the Walk

Book 5: Hooking Captain Teeth

Table of Contents

Dedication   5

Content Warning   5

Story   8

Bonus Content from Walk the Plank   197

More Monster Brides Titles   210

About the Author   212

More Books by Marilyn Barr   213

Walk the Walk

Book 5: Hooking Captain Teeth

Chapter

1

Sabrina, 1720 AD

"Why must you judge me for picking up random men at the tavern? I don't judge you for seducing the pastor at the orphanage, and don't roll your eyes as if your attraction isn't obvious! You would trade your tentacles for him in a heartbeat," I scold my big sister, Bettina. We reach the front of Maude's dirty tavern not a moment too soon. My prim sister's diatribe churns my stomach—not with guilt—but with annoyance. I have no reason to feel guilty.

What I choose to do with my one night a month as a human is my business.

"You could spend your time doing something good for the species we mimic. The joy I receive from those children's smiling faces—"

"I get the same amount of smiles. I promise," I say with a wink that twists Bettina's face into a scowl.

Walk the Walk

Book 5: Hooking Captain Teeth

"By the time I lower my skirts back into place, every man I encounter is smiling."

"Sabrina, how could you! You've ruined yourself for your fated mate," she snaps.

My eyes roll so far, I can see the back of my red hair. I thrust the bundle of fish I carried for her onto her shoulder. After she drops me off at Maude's tavern, she will continue to the cathedral in the island's center. The kids will be thrilled to roast fish over an open fire as she tells them stories of our undersea adventures. I've watched her flirt shamelessly with a man of the cloth without guilt. Why should I feel guilty because my idea of fun is more… raucous…bawdy…lively?

Her face is red with frustration and embarrassment on my behalf. The wishy-washy pastor has brainwashed her. She should remember that we can't conceive a baby without the soulbond to make us human or our mate into a Kraken. Should I inform her that once the full moon lowers and we change back into Kraken, we shed all human ailments—including the Bube and pox? Probably not. Admitting I have contracted and shed such ailments would dig me deeper into her hole of disrepute. There is no harm in what I choose to do with my time…or what she chooses…except when she tries to choose for me.

"I'm having fun! As for my fated mate… If I find him at Maude's, he's as unscrupulous as me.

Otherwise, he will never know what I've been up to. Dancing on tables is fun. Drinking rum and flirting with the men who buy it for me until I'm three sheets to the wind—is fun. And guess what? Sex is fun too."

"Sabrina, you've grown into a horrible wench!"

"Not horrible, I'm good at it," I say with a flip of my waist-length hair over my shoulder. She presses her lips together until they are white, like the lacy collar under her chin. "I'll meet you under the pier in the morning to stash our clothes. Have fun sleeping alone on a straw mattress in the drafty chapel."

Shedding my prissy sister like an itchy coating of sand, I press through the swinging half-doors of Maude's. The smoky interior smells of cigars, spoiled ale, coconut rum, and unwashed sailors. Breathing a healthy dose into my lungs, I make my way to the bar. My hips swing with feminine sensuality as I weave between the long wooden tables and askew benches. I scan each seat for my intended targets. One to buy my drinks, one to pay for my room, and one to tip Maude so she doesn't get on me for taking customers from her working girls. At least three men will treat me tonight…make that five. My sister has soured my mood, so I'll need twice the drinks to loosen up.

"The usual, Sabrina?" asks Jamal, who tends the portion of the bar closest to the door.

"Not yet," I say with a laugh. "I haven't found

the man who will tend to me tonight."

"Put her on my tab," says a dark-haired man with a scar running from his eyebrow to his chin. He throws back his shot of rum when I give him a demure nod of gratitude, lowering my lashes over my bright, sea-green eyes.

Jamal's an easy-going landlubber and would probably fit Bettina's definition of someone appropriate for me—even if his reliable job is at Maude's. He never drinks while behind the bar, stands up for strumpets whose clients can't understand 'no' or 'not now,' and always wears a smile. His smile—and my strict don't-bugger-your-friends policy— is the reason I've never taken him to bed.

I don't touch rot. Blackened teeth, matted hair, gangrenous limbs, and yellowed fingernails are deal breakers. I won't allow a man with rot to touch me—not even to help me off the tabletop after I dance over him. With Jamal's poor dental hygiene, it's a miracle I accept drinks from him.

Lucky for me, the scarred man who offered to buy my night's drinks is moderately clean. He drops off his stool to hobble my way with his peg leg clapping the wooden floor louder than Maude's off-tune piano. Missing a leg doesn't mean he has rot…quite the opposite in my experience. If he has access to a competent ship's doctor to perform such an operation, I expect he also has access to soap. This man's growing in my favor and could be my bedfellow for the night.

"Tonight's not the night for a delicate flower to swindle drinks from pirates," he whispers in my ear. His breath is thick with alcohol and coconut milk. It fans over my bare shoulder and exposed cleavage. I feel my nipples harden at the first attention I've received in a lunar cycle.

"What if this flower isn't so delicate?" I ask with a flutter of my eyelashes. He's missing a few teeth, replaced with metal crowns. Otherwise, they're as clean as his slightly yellow fingernails.

Truth be told, I could snap this guy in half with one of my tentacles. Who's he calling a flower? I'd drag him to the bottom of the ocean and drown him before he knew what had happened.

"My ship's been in this harbor for two weeks, and I've dipped my stick in every well under this roof twice…except yours. You aren't one of Maude's regular girls. I doubt you are even a working girl. I bet *Daddy* is in some hacienda wondering where his little princess ran to," he says before sucking on my earlobe.

I shiver at how much I like a man to play with my ears. Too bad his sexist comments smell of rot and drop him down a notch on my list.

"No hacienda. My *daddy* isn't on this island, nor

is my keeper. You're right. I'm not one of Maude's girls. I'm my own girl," I whisper against the bottom of his chin. Yum, he smells of gunpowder and boat tar. He's a sailor—pirate or merchant. No way would a naval soldier come to the tavern out of uniform when the uniform earns them free drinks and privileges from Maude.

Patricia's Wish docked this morning. Her Captains are a she-devil and her consort. The crew is a hoard of demons. Any one of them would ruin you," he says, rubbing a proprietary hand down my back.

"How do you know I'm not one of those demons?" I toss back the end of my drink in one swallow. My sailor's pupils dilate as he watches my throat work the liquid down my gob. I have no time or interest in conversations about good and evil. If I did, I'd be at the orphanage with Bettina—all pious and boring.

As if to come to my rescue, Maude plays a livelier tune, and the real tavern girls clamor onto the stage to dance. Their singing resembles the alley cats marooned by the ships docking on this island, but it's catchy enough to tap my sailor's toe. I lead him to the end of a long table and use him as leverage to climb on top of it. With a salute to Maude, I lift my skirts to my knees and dance along. My hem flies over my sailor's head to give him a glimpse of my thighs. I wink over my shoulder at the other men at the table to prevent him from thinking we're exclusive. He blew it with his warning about demons and she-devils.

There's one she-devil in this bar, and she's me.

I twirl as the music comes to a crescendo. Time to find my next mark. Pity because that sailor smelled so good. His rot was on the inside. The men at our table are uninspiring, so I hop onto the one adjacent. Nope, they smell of yeast dough and cheese—the telltale signs of foot and lip fungus.

Next table!

I've leaped and tapped halfway around the room when a crew of pirates burst through the doors. Their leader has shiny, clean brown hair framing cold, grey eyes. His hands are red from scrubbing. Ship's doctor, if I had to guess. Behind him is a short man—no higher than the doctor's ribs—with shocking red hair and a tidy, red beard. His blue eyes twinkle with mischief, but the set of his mouth is stern. I'd say he's the enforcer—small but lethal—like a bosun, master of sails, or quartermaster. Wouldn't he be fun for a night?

Other crewmen flood in without a care in the world. They are ratline climbers, deck scrubbers, gunners, or other disposable men, based on their dependence on the short man to scout out the bar for danger. A man with a full set of metal teeth gives me a terrifying smile before heading for Jamal. Not touching that sailor for all the pearls in the sea!

Last through the swinging doors is a man with the whitest smile I've ever seen. Crystalline blue eyes clearer than the Caribbean Sea sparkle at me. The crooked hook of his nose mars the perfection of an otherwise statue-worthy face. Tall, strong, and encased in worn leather, he's built like a ratline climber but wealthier. He scans the crowd like a seasoned pirate too.

I'm blinded by lust and momentarily lose my footing. The heel of my tattered boot lodges between two planks on the table. My ankle screams as it twists with my momentum. Arms pinwheeling, my weight swings over the edge of the table. The sticky, grog-soaked floor rushes toward my face as I prepare for impact.

I thump into the strong arms of the handsome pirate whose boots are the size of boats. My hair brushes over their metal tips and tangles in the leather laces crisscrossed up his shins. Two long, clean fingers press into the side of my breast, sending lava through my veins. He's missing the middle and ring finger at the base knuckle.

"Caught me a doxie," the handsome man yells to the crowd, who laughs and cheers in response. His deep timbre rattles my bones and spreads goose-pimples over my flesh. The cold, bare flesh of my arse, exposed to the room! I fight the hem of my skirts that flipped to my shoulders during my fall. His arm supports my weight at the waist while his hand fists my skirts to keep them up. His other hand spanks me, hard. The crack rings out over the chorus of laughter. My face heats with embarrassment. I'm not drunk enough to flash the crowd!

"Unhand me, you scoundrel," I yell upside-down, earning myself a second swat. My cocktail threatens to come up again as I spin upright. I wobble as he sets me back on the table where I fell. I should smack him. I should channel Bettina and scold him.

Why am I aroused by this handsome man who can handle me like a tiny fairy but chooses to degrade me by spanking me in public? Men like him threaten my independence and right to a night of fun each month. He's the type of pirate everyone is afraid I will meet. Did they know I'd be drawn to him like a moth to a flame?

"There we go," he says with another pat on my behind. Thankfully, this time my skirts block his contact. "Back to work, wench."

It's on the tip of my tongue to save face and tell him I'm not one of Maude's girls. He must be one of the demons from *Patricia's Wish*. The smartest course would be to dance away from him and back to the condescending sailor who smelled nice. I'm too bright to be swayed by a pretty smile…a smile without a hint of rot…and perfectly manicured nails…all seven of them as clean as his smile. As my eyes search him for flaws, he runs the four fingers of his left hand through his mane of golden hair. Both his middle fingers are missing. I'm blasted with the scent of soap, gunpowder, boat tar, and an ocean breeze.

My shoulders rise and fall as I breathe him into my lungs.

A flirty remark dies on my tongue as he adjusts himself through the crotch of his leather pants. Nope. Too much. Too uncouth, too vulgar, too smarmy, too much for a part-time human like me. He's as shameless as me but with twice the firepower. Not gracing him with another second of my attention, I twirl and dance along the table to the opposite end of the brothel. I'll find a safer man to bed tonight.

I kick and tap to the beat with my skirts swishing above my knees for mediocre sailors, stealing furtive glances at the handsome man and his table of rowdy friends. I don't dare approach them. I do possess some sense of self-preservation. The night flies by as shots are taken from my cleavage and poured down my throat by random drunks.

All the while, the handsome pirate watches me from his corner.

The heat in his stare burns away my inhibitions,

and I find myself performing for him, using the attention from men closer to me as my props. Coins jingle in my pockets and shoes as I earn my night's lodgings under the pirate's lustful gaze. It isn't long before I'm singing louder than the girls on stage.

My peg-legged companion leaves with his head shaking in warning. He can't buss my cheeks. He's not my father. My father's at the bottom of the Atlantic Ocean. I thumb my nose at the swinging doors as he exits the bar.

Time to secure a room from Jamal. Looks like I'll be sleeping alone tonight, but some nights are slow. On a good night, I'll take two or three men to my room in succession before selecting the one I will sleep beside. Nights like tonight balance the scales. My body must wait another month for a masculine touch to feed my desires. I hope the working girls are luckier and wake up next to stacks of gold.

"Here's one, two, five gold coins," I count as I drop doubloons onto the bar top. Maude's rate is three coins for rooms not occupied by her girls, so the two extra coins will go to Jamal's savings. I hope he opens the beachside cantina of his dreams someday. "I'd like a room—the one at the far end of the hallway if it's open."

"Are you sure? Miss Opal has the room next to that one. Maybe take the first room," Jamal says,

Walk the Walk

Book 5: Hooking Captain Teeth

swiping my coins into his hand. He trades them for a large iron key. Being a 'screamer' is Miss Opal's specialty. I'll wake up with a banging headache if I'm in the room next to hers.

"Thanks for always looking out for me," I reply, swiping the key off the bar top.

"Which room is ours?" I don't need to turn around to know it's the handsome pirate behind me. My body ignites with the command in his question.

"I'm in room one," I say, verifying the key is labeled with the number one. He steps toward me with a palm outstretched for the key. "You are bunking in the bilge of some ship with the rest of the sea sludge."

He takes a predatory step forward. My back hits the bar. I clutch the key to my chest. It vibrates with the pounding of my heart—or maybe that's the shaking of my fingers. Blond hair tickles my nose as he leans over me, one arm resting on the bar to either side of my waist. His scent invades my nose. Blue eyes bore into me with an intensity that curls my toes in my boots.

"Tell me you don't want me in your bed to pleasure you from head to toe and make your every fantasy come true, and I'll disappear," he whispers against my ear. The brush of his lips on my earlobe unravels me.

My soul bond snaps from its cage in my heart and reaches for him.

Walk the Walk

Book 5: Hooking Captain Teeth

My fated mate stands before me.

A once-in-a-lifetime connection and the promise of true love war in my head with my common sense. He's not just a pirate, but a notoriously demonic pirate, sailing under a she-devil. For all my blustering, I'm afraid. This man will break my heart when he chooses piracy over life under the sea with me. Why would a man like him commit to a quiet life? I should save myself the agony of tying my soul to a ruffian and losing him to the sweet trade or worse.

The word 'no' will save my heart and soul.

"Stay with me," I whisper as tears gather in my eyes.

Chapter

2

Sabrina

I giggle as the handsome stranger carries me over the threshold. Even though my human form is petite, I love how dainty I feel in his arms. My ten-foot kraken tentacles are the girth of this man's leg. How will I enjoy his company without envisioning what could grow between us? He's handsome now…but as a Kraken…

Shiver.

Why must my treacherous mind go there?! When he transforms, he will be a giant Kraken with the power to sink boats with a thrash of his tentacle. I can't wait for the red flesh to propel him—and his blond locks—across the Caribbean. As a rogue pirate, I doubt he will want to remain human after our ceremony. He will give up the brothels for adventure with me; I just know it.

"You smile already, pretty lady," he says with a nuzzle where my neck meets my shoulder. "I haven't given you a reason to smile yet."

Stop it, Sabrina, before you hurt yourself!

He drops me onto the lumpy bed and pounces on me as I rebound off the musty feather mattress. Two heavy boots clunk onto the floor as he violently kicks them off. I'm practically drooling as he whips his white linen shirt over his head. His blond hair floats to his shoulders like a golden cloud. Amulets on leather cords hang from his neck to the bottom of his ribs. I follow his seven fingers as his hands smooth down his toned, lean midsection. My desire for him soars as he slowly unbuckles his belt and unties his leathers. I'm awash with shyness and snap my gaze to his face to avoid watching him remove his cock from his pants.

"You're about to miss the best part of the show, love," he says with a flick of his blue eyes downward. The cold desire in them freezes me from head to toe when our eyes meet again. He waits with his laces wrapped around his fingers until my lashes drift downward and my attention is where he directs.

I can't breathe. Any time my eyes move to a safer place—like the wall behind him—he stops. Our power play has morphed into a game of cat and mouse. Half of me wants to admit I'm in over my head and run…the other half wants to lick the ridges where his hips meet his waist. By the time his leathers hit the floor, I'm a mess of need. Usually, I'm fighting my bed partner to open my corset to fondle my breasts instead of a quick stick under my skirts. This stranger stands stark naked, stroking himself, devouring me with his eyes as if he can't decide what part of me to consume first.

My courage evaporates, and I scoot backward until my rump hits the bars of the headboard. With a deep chuckle, he crawls onto the bed, prowling toward me on all fours. My heart thunders in my chest as he grabs my ankles. He pushes them apart before pressing them down in a silent order to keep my legs open. His hands glide up my legs as he raises my skirts and slides up my clothed body. I flinch when his thumbs press the sensitive clefts behind my knees. He flashes that brilliant smile at me when he catches my tell. My cheeks heat with mortification. The skin on my inner thighs is wet with my overwhelming response to his slow seduction.

I bet he feels every drop. A calloused thumb collects the dew on my slit, and I nearly hit the ceiling. He withdraws the scandalous hand to present his shining thumb at the end of my nose. I can't look away or squirm with embarrassment. I'm pinned by his hand clasped over my cunt as I stare at how much I want him. The evidence on his hand hangs between our faces. There's nowhere to hide from my lecherous side.

His lips caress my ear as he whispers, "Sweet girl, preparing to take her captain's cock. Don't shy away from me. I'll hunt for your treasures all night if I must. It's what we scoundrels do. No need to pretend you're a blushing sweetheart with me."

As if I have an ounce of control over my body! His thumb disappears between his lips. I didn't think I could flush harder, but the heat travels from my cheeks, down my neck, and dives to my soulbeak. Below my skirts, his fingers move. He's inside me and dancing over my most sensitive tissues at the same time—doing more damage to my decorum and self-control than any other partner in my past! And he does so with fewer fingers.

"Let me hear those moans of pleasure as I learn your body." If he wants me to moan, he'll have to put in the work above my belt. I'm not a half-penny-upright who lifts her skirts for men to steal a half-minute of pleasure from her depths.

I get mine first.

"Shortgown strings," I whisper between kitten mews. Where's my voice? Where's the confident lady who had her pick of men downstairs? Who is this trembling pile of feminine need?

"These?" He removes the thumb from his mouth and grabs the strings lacing the front of my dress together. Instead of pulling the string at the bottom and allowing my bosom to slide out the top, he grips the crisscrossing lattice and pops the strings. My whalebone stays burst open on my exhale. My breasts push my linen shift through the opening like yeasted dough. The delicate linen flutters to my waist. Sticky, humid air pets the hard points of my nipples with each breath I take.

"I can't peak without—" I'm cut off by the sensation of his fingers withdrawing from my cunt. Air slams from my lungs, pushing my gaping linen shift from my shoulders. It drapes over the edges of my open stays like window curtains. His drenched index finger coats my left nipple with my arousal before he flicks it with his tongue. My head lolls backward in bliss until I hit his hand.

"Almost," he says, cradling my head so I don't hit the headboard. He slides his opposite hand under my arse to maneuver me onto my back. My skirts twist around my waist, tugging at my soulbeak. "I've got you. Thank you for telling me about those potent little buttons. Let's get you out of this dress, so I can feast on all of you."

"No, no, I'm fine," I say, clutching my skirts to my belly. It raises them higher, so the island breeze can whisper up my open sex. Hopefully, his attention draws to my exposed thighs and away from my soulbeak. I can't be naked with this dangerous man. One bite to my soulbeak will ruin everything. He may be my soulmate, but I'm not giving my freedom to him tonight. He's a stranger. "We don't know each other."

"Everyone knows Teeth," he says with the smile that must be his namesake. "But if you want to try to hide my face beneath your skirts, who am I to argue? I'll still do unspeakable things if you ask sweetly."

My knuckles glow pink as the grip on my skirt loosens. Strumpet behavior—like keeping my dress on my person to prevent theft? Let him think what he wants as long as I'm protected. I give him a shaky smile because I don't know what to say. My usual trysts don't include conversation. I shove my mark's face in my cleavage while I ride his sugarstick to my climax. There's no seduction. There's no connection. I barely notice when he peaks because I'm absorbed in satiating my need that I've built flirting downstairs.

"Eyes on me," Teeth says with a growl. He demands my full attention. I can't even retreat into my head. I must be present and acknowledge I'm under my soulmate, who hasn't a clue. "You know I have enough virtue to deserve you but not so much to leave you wanting."

"How?" I ask as I trace a scar bisecting his left eyebrow. Luckily, he understands my breathy one-word sentences.

"Protecting those I care about, rescuing others, righting the balance between men of all colors, and respecting women in all occupations," he whispers.

Walk the Walk

Book 5: Hooking Captain Teeth

His grin opens to suck my breast inside his hot mouth. His fingers work my other nipple with the tugs and rolls I love. My back arches off the bed as he works me into a frenzy. The brush of his fingertips up my thigh as he feasts on my dairy sets my body on fire. I push my knees open as far as I dare to stress my human form.

Oh, how I wish I could drape my tentacles over the sides of the bed to welcome his cock into my pelvic pouch!

His mouth wandering to the underside of my breast is like a bucket of cold water thrown over my head. He won't be the first man I've shoved off my belly before he consumes my soulbeak. I suck in my stomach as my body recoils.

"Ticklish belly, eh?"

No, but whatever works to keep him from tying us before I can explain.

"Other parts of me are more interesting," I say between gulps of air. Fear combines with lust and arousal until my mind is a jumble. It's too much, and if I don't climax soon, I'll succumb to overstimulation. I thought I had control of the human sexual sensations in this form, but I'm losing my grip on them.

"Show me," he says, raising a blond eyebrow. He's a fast learner because his fingers return to their delicious torture of my nipples that I love. "Don't frown at me, love. Show me what I'll find more interesting than your soft belly."

He shifts to the side when I bend my knees. I roll my skirts into a neat bundle at my waist, so I'm bare to our gazes below them. Maintaining eye contact, I allow my knees to fall open like butterfly wings. My fingers pull open my outer labia.

"Beautiful," he whispers with a huff as if I punched him in the stomach. Everything else is forgotten as his singular focus takes him below my waist.

He feasts on my flesh as if he's starving and I'm the last exotic fruit on a deserted island. I play with my breasts until I scream my climax. Opal screams down the hall as if we are competing to bring down the thatched roof. I shiver with aftershocks as my inner muscles squeeze his finger.

I want more but don't have the voice to ask. I'm formulating my request in my head when his arm snakes under my lower back. My back bows as I'm lifted from the bed to sit on his lap. I flop like a rag doll over his shoulder as he lowers me onto his cock. The rubbing on my inner walls and how he hits that secret spot inside me detonates a second climax. I'm seeing stars as he thrusts into me from below.

My ankles cross at the base of his spine as my eyes cross with pleasure. I wrap my arms around his strong shoulders and hold on for dear life. The undulating of his muscles against my skin is a soothing massage, caring for the nerve endings he set on fire. I find the strength in my legs to counterthrust and raise myself a few inches to fall onto him. He rocks back so my pelvis tilts and my clit rubs against him.

I peak again, and this time my ears ring as if I'm diving into the deepest ocean trench.

He drops me onto the bed a heartbeat before he roars his release. It splashes onto my stomach, zapping my soulbeak like lightning. My hand flutters over my heart in a vain attempt to calm it before it thunders out of my ribs. I exhale to the ceiling with a satisfied sigh…

…until his tip notches the top of my opening.

"You didn't think that's all I wanted from you, did you?"

We wring every droplet of pleasure from one another and, after a short nap, exhaust one another again. Throughout the night, we engage in screaming contests with our neighbors. My boldness grows as the liquor I consumed wears off, and I lose myself in the man of my dreams. He's raunchy and shameless, but surprisingly, gentle and generous. We whisper sweet promises and share dreams of a future while our connection grows from mere physical to emotional. Our souls connect as intended with my kind.

Despite our closeness, I hold onto my soulbeak. Teeth mentions marriage several times, and I suspect his ingestion of my soulbeak should be part of the ceremony. For now, I enjoy learning our human forms—in case he chooses for us to keep them as we love one another forever.

Sabrina

"Morning," I say to the blond mop beside me. It's not fair a man should sport such lush, thick hair. However, the bulging muscles along his back aren't pretty at all. No, they remind me of the power and masculinity he displayed during our night of passion. Is it too soon to tell him the truth…that we will get hitched on land before I drag him under the sea to start his conversion? I'm not a common girl, but a MidAtlantic Kraken. One bite of my soulbeak, and he will know all about my world.

"The sun's up," he shouts as he jumps to his feet. "Where's me britches? *Patricia's Wish* may weigh anchor without me. Captain Branko is as cross as the ratlines of Jacob's Ladder with me for feeling up

Magda. I can't be late again."

"Who's Magda?" I snap back, sitting up. The sheets fall to my waist before I clutch them to my throat, but not before I catch a whistle from Teeth.

"I missed an eyeful of dairy last night, didn't I? Don't look at me like that. I was loaded to the gunwales and don't remember a thing, but I can tell from the muss of your hair and the marks on your chest that I'm leaving another satisfied strumpet," he says with a flash of the killer smile I loved last night. After the tequila has worn off and the sun has risen, I'm not as fond of it.

I may just knock a few teeth loose.

"Leaving? We made plans last night!" I'm not begging…not really. He promised we'd be married today and start planning our lives… "You set sail today, don't you?"

"The sooner, the better," he says with a shudder. He pulls the braces over his shoulders to keep his britches in place, covering his ass in all ways. "I'd hang from a hempen necklace before letting some wench yoke me to land."

I won't cry. I won't cry. A tear falls onto the ratty, yellow sheets.

"Aww, pretty lady, don't be like that. Here," he says before flicking a doubloon onto the bed. "I've got an extra coin for you—just because I like your face…and what hangs beneath it. Cheer up and get ready for your next man. I'll parlay in this town again before you know it, and we will do the horizontal dance all night."

I nod because what can I say? There's no next man because I don't work at Maude's tavern? I'm not a strumpet, but I play one once a month to get my laughs from the land-people. He dons his coat, tosses his hair, and throws me a wink before leaving.

Not a kiss goodbye. I'd bite his tongue off anyway…

Chapter 3

Teeth

"Enough playing around," Chub growls. Sadistic little troll is never any fun. "Magda expects us back on board before nightfall. We're sailing up the Atlantic, and she wants to be north before the hurricane blows through. There's no time for fortune tellers when hunting your fortunes on the high seas."

"Come on, Chub," I yell at me hearty. I thought my best friend's transition from Blackbeard's quartermaster to our friends' quartermaster would make him less of a stick in the mud. My mistake. "Aren't you curious? Or are you scared your lady love is a grouchy troll like you?"

"This troll wants to live long enough to meet his lady troll," Chub quips. "What happens when you're late again? Blackbeard sliced off your fingers. What Magda cuts off, you will miss more than your marriage finger."

"I'd face the she-devil a thousand times to gaze

at the face of my lady love once," I say. Chub's eyebrows disappear into his cloud of red hair at my conviction. "Honest as the sun promises to rise tomorrow. If the wrinkly prune inside that tent can give me a glimpse of my lady fair within a crystal ball, I'll swear off brothels. I won't need to search them because I'll know her face anywhere."

"Seems to me," Chub says with a mischievous twinkle in his eyes, "if you spent more time looking above the girls' skirts instead of under them, you'd found your lady at a brothel already."

"Nah, she's not a penny brasser. I can feel she's *more*—"

"Be careful, me hearty," Chub scolds, wagging a stout finger under my nose. "The Caribbean has a different definition of more—one you can't handle."

"In the time we've spent arguing, her line's cleared."

"I hate you sometimes," Chub grouses but steps off the dusty island path.

We weave through the crowded street fair to the tent decorated in stamped moons and stars. The throng of people parts as I swagger against the tide of traffic. Chub pulls back the tent flap and disappears into the darkness. I flick my hands to shake off the fear and bad juju wafting from the mystic's dwelling.

Inside, the energy is just as uncomfortable, like

the matting of my chest hair from the humidity onto my sunburn with no relief in sight. A round table carved from a purple rock dominates the space. I'm compelled to hold my tongue or at least keep my voice respectfully quiet. The rock setup is too close to an altar for my liking.

Just as I predicted, the fortune teller has more wrinkles than a furled sail. She remains seated at the table with her hands perched over a crystal ball as we enter—ol'bat doesn't even open her eyes. We could slit her throat, haul her crystal table to the boat, break it down into bags of gems, and weigh anchor before anyone was the wiser. As someone who can supposedly tell the future, shouldn't she foresee the menace of two of *Patricia Wish's* top sailors in her tent? I don't know whether to be annoyed or upset at her easy demeanor.

"I like you," she croaks in a ghostly voice. Her hoop earrings sway as she looks over us. A musical clinking under her fluttering sleeves accompanies her movements. "You've come looking for love and not riches."

"Love is riches—more so than all the gold in the Caribbean," Chub murmurs. He lays his sheathed machete on the table as a sign of peace. I follow his lead and plop into the remaining empty chair. It groans in protest as my lanky frame sprawls out in the remaining space. My sheathed longsword and small satchel of doubloons thump onto the table.

"We're willing to pay for a glimpse of our lady loves," I whisper, not breaking eye contact with the creepy gray orbs boring into my skull. "What's your price?"

"You won't pay the price for love, but your friend will—"

"What do you mean? Will I lose a finger, my life, my face—" Chub sits up in alarm as his fears blast from his gob like cannon fire.

"No, you won't pay the price for love either," the fortune teller says with a chuckle. "The one who loves the night will pay in sweet trade to be with her soulmate in the darkness."

"She means Captain Branko and Magda the Vampiress," I console Chub, who probably already figured out the riddle. Branko wants to retire as a farmer with Magda, so giving up the sweet trade— piracy—to live in darkness is exactly what he wants.

"Aye, but what about us? Will we have to pay a price?"

"A Doubloon per card," she croaks, but her voice has changed. Her eyes weren't brown a minute ago...weren't they gray? She fusses with the billowing, black sleeves of her gown to reveal her gnarled hands and vein-crossed wrists. If she's not wearing bracelets, where's the clinking coming from? "Each card will reveal a secret about your lady love. The more you want to know…the more you pay—"

"Pay in doubloons, aye? I'm not signing up to servitude," Chub growls. His fear raises the hair on my arms. Chub's job as a quartermaster is to think ahead and scout for danger. If he's worried, I better run for the docks.

"This doesn't harm our spirits or souls, right?" Not that I believe she would give me an honest answer, but my question gives Chub time to assess the trouble we've invited and decide whether to proceed. My heart pounds in my throat harder than when I squared off with Blackbeard without flinching —and lost a few fingers for my trouble.

"For information? No, karmic servitude or spiritual repercussions. I promise. Those are for trying to change someone or the future. You want to see your ladies, not lure them to you, so your souls are safe," she says in the same voice. I watch her eyes for a color change as they dart between us. I'm disappointed when they stay violet…wait, they were brown, right?

"What island holds my lady love?" Desperation pulls the questions from my lips.

The crystal ball glows with swirling smoke. The fortune teller leans closer. Chub and I lean so close, we make four nostril clouds on the glass. "I should see the landscape, but all I see are empty waves," I say with a hollow chuckle.

"She's not on an island. In fact, she's not on land," the fortune teller says to the beat of clinking bracelets. The constant noise must annoy her after a long day. "You'd be better searching for her on the high seas, but that doesn't give you the information you seek."

"I want to see her," I murmur. Honesty leaks from my mouth like a breach in the hull. Brown-eyed Crone must have bewitched me.

While my mind struggles with eye colors and phantom bracelets, the fortune teller lifts her crystal ball from the table. I swear it hovers in midair before slowly drifting to the floor on its own. My face remains blank while my guts churn like stormy seas. This prune is the real deal.

The black cards slap and scrape as she shuffles them. Her fingers shouldn't be able to move so fast. I didn't think she could straighten them. Cards fly from one hand to another. Each time the deck stops to be sorted, the design changes from stars, to fish, to hearts, to demons with glowing red eyes. I'm a heartbeat from grabbing me hearty by the britches and hauling him out of the tent when she fans the plain, green cards in front of him.

"Of all the hornswoggle," he grouses. He reaches

for the top card when the prune gasps.

"Don't pull too quickly," she says, grabbing his wrist. Chub rears back in his seat but can't dislodge his beefy hand from her curled fingers. "Run your hand over them. Feel the energy of her heart calling to you. Select the card that wants to speak to you."

"Cards can't talk, ye pudding-headed buzzard," he gripes, yanking his hand away. She holds steady while his blue eyes blaze with icy rage. She guides his hand back and forth, an inch over the fan of cards. "Maybe two of them buzz like rope burn."

"There you go," she says with a grin minus her top teeth. "Pick up the two cards and toss me two doubloons from your bag."

I toss her the coins while Chub flips over two cards from the fan. The first card is near the top, with ten tentacles waving from the edges to the center. The second card is right in the middle of the deck. Chub growls at the giant spider staring back at him from an intricate web. I turn the spider card to face me and break the tension between Chub and the drawing. Sure enough, the spider is smiling. *Huh?* Chub's lady love is a happy spider?

"Before you allow your rage to destroy my tent, please listen to their meaning. The tentacles signify riches—true diamonds—your lady love is quite wealthy. Do you know any wealthy ladies from the

Pintarro, Brown, or LeFaire families? Those are the only families in the Caribbean with enough riches to inspire ten tentacles."

"That no good Pintarro has been a thorn in our sides for years," Chub says with a chuckle. "There's no way he'd surrender the bonnie Catalina Pintarro to a pirate. What's the spider?"

"Her," the fortune teller snaps.

Chub's smile falls from his face. "In one breath, you say my lady love is a wealthy lady—the most bonnie of prizes, and in the next, you call her a blimey bug?!"

"I don't call her anything. It's the spirits."

"Smite your spirits and curse their descendants," Chub says, rising from his chair. "Let's cast aboard, Teeth. It's nearly sundown and time to weigh anchor. I want to nap off this experience before I'm to steer us from port."

"But that's only one lady," the fortune teller whispers in a sultry, feminine voice. Long lashes flutter over the bright, sea-green eyes sunken into the old hag's face. "Don't you want a peek?"

"I'm not afraid," flies out of my mouth. Chub pauses by my side and clasps my shoulder. The silent command for me to stay and draw my cards is heard as loud as if he shouted it. "Just one glimpse. Not two cards that will argue with themselves or three to break a tie; I want one card with one message. That's all my simple mind can handle—"

"Not your mind, but your heart is what can handle the lady who burns for you." Avast ye! The fortune teller's eyes are gorgeous. I could get lost in them. And to hear my lady burns for me without knowing me? My shaft stands to half-mast, ready to extinguish the inferno in my britches that has nothing to do with the fireship who infected me last night.

"Where are you?" I whisper as I run my hand over the cards in the same manner she taught Chub. The corner of a card catches on the stump of my former marriage finger. It flips out of the array and bounces into my lap. With trembling fingers, I pluck it from the gap between my erection and my belt. "Little lady has an appetite in the sheets to match mine!"

"Blimey, man, that's your future wife! Have some respect!" Chub scolds me with a slap to the back of my head.

The momentum sends me forward, and the card tumbles from my hand. It settles into my view as if presenting itself like a dinner plate. A bright red octopus stares at me with squinting eyes and menacing teeth. Blooming beasty looks ready to jump from the paper to rip my face off. I don't know whether to be excited or terrified. My lady love could be as monstrous as Magda with twice the arms to dodge.

"Right," Chub says, flipping a doubloon at the black-eyed witch who conned us into a card reading. "If ten tentacles mean a wealthy lady, me hearty will marry the fecking Queen of England! We're done here."

"He knows his lady love—"

"I've never met the Queen of England."

"King George the First rules England," the fortune teller says, rubbing her eyes with exasperation.

"I haven't met him either!"

"Time to board, matey," Chub announces, squeezing my shoulder. "You won't find her in this tent. Best keep to the seas and build a fortune to house her…especially if your queen requires a castle."

"She doesn't require a castle—she's not royalty. That's not what the cards are trying to tell you. You've met your lady love before—"

"Great," I snap, rising from my seat. "We had our chance and blew it? Story of my life."

Chapter

4

Captain Teeth, 1725 AD
Five years later

"With a t-wink-le in his eye and a s-song in her heart, they sailed into the s-s-sunset," I read with pauses too long and accents askew. "I bet he had a twinkle in his eye after she emptied his bollocks in chapter four. This may be my favorite book yet."

"Aye, Captain, I'm proud of you," says Chub, my quartermaster and best friend. "You read that book in nye under a week. Last summer, it would've taken you a week to figure out a paragraph's worth of words."

"I have a great teacher," I say with a clap to his shoulder. Each evening as the sun sets and he takes his shift at the helm, he teaches me to read. Reading is one of the many things I've learned since becoming Captain of *Patricia's Wish*. Only the patience and cunning of me hearty could bring me to the level befitting the crew in such a short amount of time. "A steady supply of bawdy books has helped too."

"A pathetic excuse for the real thing," Chub says in an exaggerated tone that suggests his lady love has stepped on deck. "Nothing is as fine as resting one's head over his lady's heart."

His fiancé, Catalina, doesn't usually join us for our reading lesson since she's busy cleaning up after our evening meal in the galley. She sails with our sorry lot for Chub, but as soon as we dock in Mexico, they will leave the sweet trade for their next adventure. I'll miss them terribly, but I couldn't be happier for me best matey.

From a street rat in Ireland to quartermaster under Blackbeard, he worked his way into a fortune before boarding *Patricia's Wish.* Together, the couple has more money than sense. Blimey, why the richest lady in the Caribbean stays on as a ship's cook and not a guest is beyond me.

"Over his lady's heart, buss my cheeks! You mean resting your head on your lady's dairy," she says with a cheeky smile.

"Easy for you to say. You have each other," I grouse. I face the ocean to miss the kissing and groping as the couple greets one another. A flat, calm sea with a pink sky overhead is exactly what a sailor wants to see. We will have nice weather.

"The last brothel we visited—the one in St.

Kitts—was it me, or were the wenches younger than ever? Half of them I was too scared to touch. What if their fathers came after me? The other half, I wanted to feed them and read a bedtime story to tuck them into bed. Not a one could raise my mizzenmast—" This was the first time I've had a problem bedding wenches. After I returned to the captain's quarters, I tested my plumbing. Thank goodness it was shipshape.

"—And that's saying something," Chub interrupts as the happy couple laughs at my expense. Catalina's herbal potions have cured more than a couple of ailments within me britches, so there's no hiding my love of brothels and their employees.

"Maybe you are done with brothels?" Catalina asks with a shy smile.

"I fear me hearty has caught the ennui," Chub replies.

"I haven't itched for weeks!"

"I can attest he hasn't," Catalina says. "My oregano plants are thriving. It's exciting to use them for more than tinctures."

"Ennui," Chub explains after he yanks the wheel to the left to correct the rudder. "Ennui is a plague of the spirit. It's when a pirate tires of the sweet trade and life in general. It's a type of loneliness."

He's right. Pretending to check the hull over the railing, I flick my tears into the drink. It takes a few sniffs and a pull from my hipflask to bury my *ennui* where my friends can't see it. I can't help the pang of jealousy when I turn back to them. Catalina's arms loop around Chub's neck as she nestles against his side. His left arm cradles her while his right steers the ship's wheel. I have no interest in Catalina, but I'd give a few of my infamous teeth to have my lady love cuddled under my arm.

"You're looking for your lady love in the wrong places, matey."

"I don't expect to find her in a brothel," I shout, throwing my hands in the air. "The wenches are just to scratch the itch until she arrives."

"Seems to me the brothels give more itches than scratches," Catalina says with a giggle.

"What I meant was you've been looking for a human woman when this boat has a history with women who are *other*," Chub says, kissing Catalina's temple to show me where I've gone wrong.

"Why? Because the ship was first captained by Magda the Vampiress?"

"The Vampiress who stole our pal Branko's heart," finishes Chub. "Why else would he resign to become a landlubber on a godforsaken island? I'm about to leave the sweet trade for Catty, too."

"I don't think our sweet Catalina can be compared to Magda the She-devil."

"Oh yeah?" Catalina says with a fire igniting in her brown eyes. In the span of a heartbeat, she unfurls the leather cuffs from her spinnerets and sprays ten fibers at me. I don't dare move a muscle as the nearly translucent threads wrap around my neck. If either of us jumps in alarm, she may strangle me. She makes ropes strong enough to hold the weight of two crewmen. But before she joined us, her spinnerets made all the lace in Europe, but she abandoned the Pintarro Textile Empire for Chub's embrace.

"You could use Catty's mortar and pestle to track down your lady love. The thing has magic from the old country," Chub suggests, rubbing his red beard. When he rubs his beard, it's usually because he's devising a cunning plan where I'm the decoy or bait. Such is the life of a Captain—we are nothing more than cannon fodder in floppy hats and brightly colored jackets.

"Oh no," I say through clenched teeth so I don't jostle the threads on my jaw. "No more magic. Not after that horrendous card reading in St. Kitts."

"My bowl isn't some parlor trick like a crystal ball," Catalina says, whipping her fibers off me. They coil around the railing of the sterncastle deck before the ends flip into the open hands of their owner. She uses her fingers to weave them into a complicated lace pattern with lightning speed. Maybe I underestimated her *other* nature. "That mortar and pestle told me who my soul mate was, told him that I was his—and tells me what to feed you each day. Its magic is real."

"I don't doubt magic, the existence of *other*s, or that the devil walked on the earth as Blackbeard. You don't understand my terror when the crone pulled out her cards after her crystal ball showed nothing," I say, pacing the small platform of our sterncastle deck.

"Nothing? Some fortune teller," Catalina says with a tsk.

"I asked what nation held my lady love, and the crystal ball glowed with swirling smoke. The fortune teller said I should see the landscape, but all I saw were empty waves," I say with a hollow chuckle.

"So, she read your cards?"

"Yep, I asked her haunted deck to show me my lady love—" I pause to swallow my terror at the memory "—wanted to see the smile of my firecracker. Somewhere in this world is my match. I know the fire in her heart, but I wanted to know her face. I thought it was too much to ask for the direction I must travel."

"Aye, I bet she's as playful as a breeze but strong as a hurricane," Chub says with a look of pity scrunching his features. If anyone understands my loneliness, it's him. We inherited the boat from Magda and Branko to find love…not treasure.

He won. So far.

"Yeah, that's the kill devil," I say, squeezing the railing until my knuckles whiten. "Old prune pulled the card of an octopus."

"Octopus is the ace of diamonds, you nutmeg," Chub says with a laugh. "Your lady love is an heiress like me Catty, squirreled away in an island hacienda."

"I'd like to think that," I say, looking at my seven knuckles. "But you said it first, this boat has a habit of attracting *others*. What if I'm to meet the mighty Kraken who sinks boats all over the Atlantic? What if it's an omen that I will find peace at the bottom of the sea?"

"Nobody is meant to die alone," Catalina says, clutching her half-woven lace to her chest.

"Listen here, cup-shot pudding head, you can't be sunk to the bottom of the Atlantic Ocean by some demonic squid for two reasons. The first—our course is west to Mexico with the Atlantic at our backs. The second—we've flown overboard more times than I can count. The sea always spits us back onto land. The Caribbean doesn't want the likes of us littering her seafloor."

"Devil take me," I say, chuckling with my hands over my face.

"He didn't want our sorry arses either," Chub says with a loud guffaw. "Ol' Blackbeard marooned us years ago. That's how we ended up sailing under

Magda—"

"And yet you stayed to sail under me. You've been quartermaster under all three of us. I appreciate you sticking by me," I say with a clap to his shoulder. "No use both of us walking the night. I won't sleep until morning with Vampire Magda's ways still in my bones. Why don't you and Catalina retire? I'll take a turn at the helm."

"Mighty kind, Captain," Catalina says, winding the end of her threads into a ball to take her project down to the officer's quarters by the infirmary. The blasted happy couple has the room beneath the captain's cabin, so their near-wedded bliss rattles my windows. "She's out there, you know. Your lady love dreams of you right now; I just know it."

"Dreaming of wringing your neck with her tentacles," Chub quips. He ducks my swat to the back of his head—not an amazing feat since he's two feet shorter than me.

"Not funny. If she sinks me boat, you'll be in Davy Jones's locker next to me," I say with a laugh.

I wave off the happy couple and take the helm. *Patricia's Wish* sails into the sunset like the boats in my books, but I stand alone at the wheel. Where's the wench to nestle under my arm and squeeze my bicep? Is it too much to ask for a companion to laugh at my jokes, sing bawdy songs, and dance between the sheets? The gulls quiet, and a hush descends over the Caribbean. Nothing but the gentle lap of the waves—

And Catalina's cries of ecstasy. *Bloody hell.*

Why couldn't I find my wife first? My jealousy of my quartermaster will worsen before it gets better. As captain, I must officiate their wedding. Chub wrote down what to say when he officiated Branko and Magda's wedding. Can I read his scribble without sounding like a pudding head? I should read the passages nightly to get the words down. I'll be a hurricane of emotions during the ceremony, which will throw a storm over my focus.

I won't just be joining them in holy matrimony. I'll be releasing my best mate from his post and the sweet trade. Chub the pirate will become Ellis the husband, farmer, and father. While I'm trapped in a marriage with the sea…and whatever tentacled beast swims in the abyss, he will retire to land.

Abandoning my post at the wheel, I stomp to the railing and glare at the pretty pink sunset. I keep a bottle of high-class rum tied to this section of railing for her…my lost love. The half shot of firewater burns as it dribbles down my throat. I pour the other half of the shot into the sea in the hopes it will find its way to her lips.

"Where the hell are you, love? Why must you torture us by hiding from your intended? I know I promised to scour the world and travel all her seven seas to find you, but I didn't think you'd put me to the test! Just appear in my life, and I'll change into whatever it takes to make you happy!"

Chapter 5

Sabrina

"Oh, I get it now," Bettina says from behind me. Drat! I didn't lose her around the Bahama Islands. "I knew if I followed you into the Caribbean, I would end up under a pirate ship."

"And when I follow you on land, will I end up under a pastor?"

"I hate you sometimes, Sabrina," she says, crossing her front two tentacles under her seaweed-wrapped breasts. Funny how many human gestures she uses in her Kraken form. She even covers herself with makeshift clothes when nobody under the sea cares. It's almost as if her heart has convinced her to become human when she bonds with her soulmate.

"No, you don't," I say with a sigh. "Help me cut this line. Teeth's alone at the helm. If I cut the anchor loose, the boat will drift for hours before he knows what happened."

"How many anchors has he lost since you met

him?"

"Seven, but I'm not counting," I say as my blade saws through a deceptively strong strand. Where do they buy rope like this? I've never seen threads so thin yet stronger than a shark's bite. While my hands busy themselves with the rope, I use six tentacles to dig the sand out from under the anchor. "Don't tell me you're worried about a few rogue pirates when boats fill our seas like sandfleas."

"No, I'm worried my little sister fell for a pirate and will likely get herself hurt."

"Too late," I reply, bunching my tentacles around me in a comforting ball. The water temperature dropped. I'm cold, not sad. *Yeah right.* "He rejected me years ago and broke my heart. I'm not swooning over him. I'm plotting his demise."

My sister's smart enough to let it go but doesn't reach for her knife to help me. This conversation has played itself during every season of every year since Teeth mistook me for a half-penny-upright in a seedy brothel. Should I have chased him despite the waning period of my human form? If I'd run to his ship, I could have turned into my Kraken form on the deck. My fear of Magda, the she-devil captain, and further humiliation kept me tangled in our musky sheets. Would I have had the strength to defend myself if Teeth rejected me and I was forced to battle a vampiress in my Kraken form? Or would they have welcomed me with open arms as Teeth's soulmate and an *other*?

I'll never know.

The sawing of my knife slows as tears gather in my eyes. My arms are as sore as my gills. The sunset faded into the night while I worked my blade. The clear skies clouded with threats of rain. I've struggled with this anchor for hours. Even the sand pit I dug isn't deep enough to free it. I misjudged the size of the rock they used for mooring. The new rope may defeat me.

He may defeat me.

"He won't love you if you kill him, you know," Bettina says with a prissy hum. "Murder will send you to hell—"

"Which is where a murdering pirate will go too," I shout, venting my frustration at the nearest—not the intended—target. Thunder cracks overhead. "I'll make our world safer by murdering his crew, so don't spit your pastor's sermons at me. It's not like Teeth will smile down on us from heaven, knowing I rot in hell. How do you think he rose to captain on a she-devil's boat—charity work? Feeding the poor? Half the bastards in the orphanage you tend are probably his. I didn't get a miracle worker for a soulmate. Now, will you help me sink his boat or not?"

"Fine, he's awful—even too awful for you.

When will you let him go? Why let hate cloud your heart if you never intend to confront him?"

"Because the soulbond snapped into place the night we met." My shouts turn to sobs as I sheathe my knife onto my belt. Bettina gathers me into her embrace and pets my hair. When my wails calm to tiny hiccups, she holds me at arms-length. I lower my tentacles to give her a clear view of the soulbeak over my belly. The tiny scale is smaller than my thumb but holds my soul's tether. "I've had a hundred opportunities to sink his boat or throw him into the sea every hurricane season, but I right his ship to safety every time the waves tip it too far."

"You still have your soulbeak, or you would be human. Why do you think your soulbond is in place with him?"

"Sounds strange, but where usually a soulmate must eat the soulbeak before we lose ourselves, I'm drawn to this man. My passionate feelings for him frighten me. If it's not sorrowful longing, it's blazing hatred. I know the bond isn't in place, but I feel like a part of me sails up there."

"I understand," she whispers, gathering me into her arms again.

"You do?" I'm so confused. Bettina and passion are opposites, like sunrise and sunset.

"My feelings for Pastor Richard are as scary and

wild as a ship on fire, blazing over the ocean. Hatred and love aren't opposites. Trying to ignore your feelings will give them the space to burn out of control. You must acknowledge them and pray to release them—"

"Oh, for Pete's sake," I yell, pushing her away. "Stop parroting him! Don't you have an independent thought left, or did he crowd them out with his rhetoric? Thanks for your help, but no thanks."

Sand kicks up around me as I push off the bottom of the ocean. I spray ink at Bettina as I glide toward the surface at full speed. Bright yellow fish, Kraken snacks, flap their tails as they scurry out of my path. Sleeping manatees roll at speeds I didn't think they could achieve. Did the current pick up? The shadows of sharks in the distance change their paths to follow the yellow fish…and away from my cloud of ink. Nothing like murky darkness to scare away a predator who hunts by sight!

If only Teeth didn't have a handsome smile, muscular body, and smooth voice. He wouldn't attract the attention of ladies who hunt by sight. The bastard would rely on the working girls like the rest of his scurvy lot. If he lost his teeth, would he still be Teeth? I'd be doomed anyway. That's the nature of my kind's stupid soulbond. Kraken carried soulbeaks before the advent of brothels, taverns, pirates, or scurvy. If Teeth is mine, then fate would find a way to bring us together. He would hurt me no matter what his face looked like or his chosen occupation.

He took one look at me and saw me as less than a person.

Well, nobody humiliates a Kraken.

I breech the surface with an obnoxious splash. The truth smacks my face with the cool, salty air. I'm hopping mad because I'm mad at myself...and Bettina was right. I'll dive into a fishing net before I admit it to her, but years of meaningless sex was my downfall—not because I caught the Bube. I caught feelings for my destined mate when he assumed the night we shared was meaningless fun. More than a soulbond, I like him. He's wild, adventurous, and progressive enough to allow me to be wild at his side. I'm jealous of every woman on his boat—even the one who scrubs the poop deck.

I can't let him go, and I hate it. My heart thunders behind my hand as I lean against the hull of his ship. Someone may see me, but I take the risk every night. If he stopped yelling into the void for his lady love, my heart would shatter. His absence would mean he's found someone else. As long as he's as miserable as me, we are in balance...and I don't want to kill him.

"Where are you, love? Another sunset, and I still haven't crossed paths with you," Teeth calls from the railing above me. He hiccups. Blimey, he's halfway into his bottle already. "I brought you a drink. I hope you're a drinker. If not, I'm sorry you're paired with a grog-blossom like mine. Of course, I'd give up the drink for you. I'd give up almost anything to make you happy…wherever you are."

Even the storm clouds brewing overhead can't overshadow Teeth. He doesn't wear a colorful coat or fluffy hat like the other captains I know. Blond hair whips around his head, down to his elbows. His leathers are the same worn clothing he wore when we met years ago. He may have climbed the status ladder, but he's humble—or no richer than when he was a ratclimber in the rigging.

My heart softens for the man the more I study him. Lightning crisscrosses the sky above him, but he doesn't flinch. One strike would sink his boat, but he's at ease. Does he not fear his death? I'd love to ask him. Not lightning, hurricanes, boarding enemy vessels, nor devil captains scare Teeth. He's larger than life, but who's the man beneath the leather, tattoos, and scars?

"How can you be so cruel?" Bettina whispers as she surfaces beside me. I put my finger to my lips to shush her, but Bettina never stops. Hopefully, the splats of rain on the deck will disguise her whispering. "The words of love you desire are said by the man you desire."

"You'd be proud of me, love. I finished another book with Chub's help. It was a Christmas love story—oh. Do you celebrate Christmas? We don't celebrate on the boat because most of me hearties aren't Christians. The sects won't baptize the likes of us—with our drinking, premarital relations, and acceptance of all people. You see, love, my crew will love you—no matter your skin color, worship habits, or even your choice of drink! Hell, Magda drank a man's blood if she fancied him, and the crew loved her," he says with a laugh and another hiccup.

"How dreadful!" Bettina's whisper is a heartbeat before Teeth pours his "mate's drink" into the sea and over her head. Bettina sinks to rinse the booze from her hair. I submerge myself in the hopes the saltwater will dampen my laughter.

"Stay close to the hull where he can't see you."

"He doesn't know you're listening," Bettina whispers with squinting eyes and shaking head. "He speaks to a mystery woman when you're right under his nose."

"Every night." Tears run into my mouth when I speak. How long will we torture one another? Am I hurting myself by punishing him? Thunder answers me.

"He can't be a heartless rogue *and* share a drink with the love of his life every night. Still, he's a pirate, and tying your eternal soul to a pirate isn't wise," she says, wiping rainwater from her brow.

"He's all bluster," I grouse.

"For who's benefit? He's alone on deck and doesn't know we're here. Aren't you afraid of rot? Hating him will rot you from the inside out."

"And tempting a man of the cloth into premarital sex with a Kraken is pure as sea foam?"

"Fine," she says, pushing off the hull. "I don't have to take this abuse from you. See you in the deep."

"Wait, I'm sorry!" I call after her, but she disappears into the dark water.

"Who's there? Who dares to sneak up on *Patricia's Wish*? Climb our Jacob's Ladder, and you'll meet the sharp end of my sword—for you have interr...interr…" Teeth's declaration is interrupted by the crashing of iron against the deck before he can remember the word interrupted. Poor drunk Captain—

Splash.

My dreams come true when Teeth falls head over heels into the sea. Unfortunately, he's too drunk to recognize me. His brow lowers as he struggles to focus on my face. The building seas toss him. Thirstier than a fish, his mouth gapes for air, swallowing gallons of saltwater. One minute, I'm staring into his glazed eyes, and the next, his blond mane swirls on the waves.

He will surface any moment now. He's not

tricking me into touching him. Touching him is dangerous. I refuse to let go of my anger. I'll wait for his ruse to end and buss his cheeks for faking his death. Not funny. As bubbles rise and pop where he disappeared, my mind quiets.

Is he too drunk to swim?

Pride be damned, I never wanted him to die! I dive under the waves. The Caribbean Sea is pitch black without the lingering sunset or churning sand to glitter in puffs. Even my enhanced Kraken sight with double eyelids isn't enough to discern shadows from sharks. Teeth's golden hair and shiny weapons make him a lighthouse. He's a target for any sight predator.

Barracuda. Sharks. Jacks. Snappers. They can't have him. He's mine.

Walk the Walk

Book 5: Hooking Captain Teeth

Chapter

6

Captain Teeth

The grog from Aruba is no holy water. It's gone to my head and messed with my innards. One moment, I'm swashbuckling on the deck, and the next, I'm in the drink—and not the potent potable kind. I fall face-first into the ocean. Come on, arms, move! Legs, kick! Waist, bend! Some part of me must fight the current before I drink the Caribbean. Each gulp of air yields the salty taste of certain death.

Like my rascally crew, my body won't obey my orders. Would my arms swim if Chub were to yell at them like the nutmegs on our ratlines?

How easy would it be to sink to Davy Jones's locker? I've drunk more seawater than grog tonight.

Chub and Catalina run the boat. I'm just a figurehead. Captains are nothing more than targets for boarding enemies, harbormasters, soldiers, cannonballs, and crew members with grievances. I haven't been given a black spot because no one else wants the job. Another gulp of ocean slides down my gullet. If I drown tonight, the boat will sail the same tomorrow as it did today. They'll miss me for a journey or two—maybe write a bawdy ballad about Ol'Captain Teeth's sparkling smile or missing fingers. Me hearties are the closest I have to family, so remembrance in a drinking song is the best memorial I can hope to achieve.

If I close my eyes…

"No," says a feminine voice beside me.

Is that a mermaid? I'd call her a siren, but the husky whisper isn't a sweet song. Plus, protesting my drowning would be bad for business if she were a siren luring me to my death. I'm not a learned man, but I've wrestled the sweet trade since my teens. Death and business are my areas of expertise.

Let me go, wench.

"You can't die," she says when I resurface. "I won't allow you to die."

Her red hair tangles around my arms and legs. She hugs my waist to hold me afloat. How can she reach me from a yard away? I sink below the surface to collect an eyeful of dairy. Topless in stormy seas at night without another boat in sight? Maybe she is an imaginary mermaid conjured by rum. The flash of a shark's belly could resemble the creamy swells of breasts in the murky deep. Maybe my destiny is shark food.

Doesn't that take the biscuit?

How much seawater must I drink to lose consciousness and end this? I've lived a thousand lives—and cheated death twice as many times—since I stepped onto Blackbeard's boat. Lost my birthname, my fingers, my virginity—I don't remember in what order. I'm done with this lonely world. Is it too much to ask to be gone before I must leave Chub to his happy life on land?

"Stop making yourself heavy," she scolds me as she drags me closer to her. How can her hair be so strong? "You can swim, imbecile, I've seen you—"

My ship groans in response to her captain leaving his post. She lists away from us as if turning a cold shoulder. A wave sweeps over my mermaid and me, but we resurface instantly, thanks to her powerful…hair? The boat rights itself in a quarter turn that I'm sure sent the helm spinning. She's facing north and dragging our anchor at a good clip.

"If I'm not dying, I must right the wheel. Someone must wake the crew to batten down the hatches. No storm can take *Patricia's Wish*." I twist to dislodge the mermaid's hold on me so I can return to the boat. If I can grasp Jacob's ladder on the side of the hull, I can climb aboard before the ship's wake drowns me.

Walk the Walk

Book 5: Hooking Captain Teeth

My blood runs cold when I reach to untangle the hair around my waist only to find it's a tentacle.

A large octopus tentacle. A red tentacle with the girth of my thigh.

Lightning flashes overhead to illuminate my first glimpse of my rescuer.

"Lady love," I say in awe. Layers of fiery red hair frame sea-green eyes so bright they reflect white in the storm's flickers. Her narrow shoulders and slender neck are human, but the muscular appendages wrapped around my body are *other*. She's bold, untamed, stronger than most of my mateys, but dumb enough to risk her neck to save my arse from the storm.

"If you wanted to catch a pirate, your timing is worse than half the port authorities in the Caribbean. This isn't the time or place for romance."

"I've already caught and sampled you, Teeth! You couldn't see you had your destiny in your arms when you had the chance."

"So, you know something I don't, and you think that makes you special? You pulled one over on Captain Teeth the Idiot. Well, so has everyone else! Being smarter than me doesn't make you special!"

"You wouldn't know what makes me special because you assumed I was another whore to warm your sheets! You don't even remember me!"

"I think I'd remember quiffing a Kraken!"

"I was in my human form. Blimey, you are stupid, aren't you? Not to mention you're as good as pickled in booze," she snaps.

"Don't let that steal the wind from your sails! I bet I was drunk the night we rode the St. George."

"You humiliated me!"

"I'm sorry? If I apologize, will you let me live?"

"You don't get to die," she says with a fire brighter than hell's inferno blazing in her eyes. "If I must suffer the loneliness—"

"You think I'm not lonely? I have an image to maintain, so my crew will work together to survive. A fierce captain keeps other pirates from looting the boat, the authorities from arresting us all, and troublemakers from causing a mutiny that can sink a boat. I can't be myself. I lie to everyone but Chub, and he's smitten with his intended. Loneliness is all I have…"

The waves slap at us. The rain pours in sheets. In the flashes of lightning, I study her expressions as they dance across her features. There's more than the tough exterior she wants to show me. She's a mirror of my innermost self that I hide from the world. A monster who regrets the choices of their youth because they led to an isolated existence.

"Let's save this fight for when you're not dragging us into the abyss," she says when a clap of thunder shakes the earth. "Stop squirming! In these swells, you will never make it aboard before the boat's riptide drags you under. Let's make for land, and I'll return you in the morning."

"She'll sink by morning!" I fumble with her tentacles to escape, but she's locked my wrists to my waist in several loops of muscle. She's in her element, and I'm three sheets to the wind. The pelting rain and dropping temperatures can't sober my mind fast enough.

"Better the boat than you! You can't save the boat from beyond the grave!" Strong, brave, and furious, my lady love is a force of nature. She's beautiful and borderline terrifying. As much as I'd love to allow her to carry me away, I'm Captain Teeth first. I won't abandon me hearties.

"A captain doesn't abandon his ship!"

"A kidnapped one does," she says through clenched teeth. Oh, thank the heavens, small square teeth sit between her lush lips instead of fangs. I kissed fangs in my past—not a fan of cut gums, scraped teeth, and busted lips. "Help me swim!"

"Can't paddle when you've pinned my wrists, love," I say with a smirk. She can't see my expression as she swims away, dragging me within her tentacles. I'll have to try harder to get a reaction. "Kinky, but now is not the time—"

"Kick your feet and use those abdominal

muscles to keep yourself buoyant—"

"Aye, aye," I chirp, just to see her pause to glare at me once more. My mates can't blame me for falling into the drink and being carried away by my lady love. Not only has my search for her been common scuttlebutt on the boat, but choosing quim over duty is par for the course with me. Frequenting a brothel when I was supposed to be guarding *Queen Anne's Revenge* was the reason Ol'Blackbeard cut off my marriage finger.

"If I knew I'd drag your sack of bones to shore, I'd have wished for my fated mate to be short and slender!" Her grunts and growls are precious.

How lucky am I? She recognizes me as a fated mate, so we can skip the song and dance where I must convince her I'm the one. I hate cream pot love and the dumb things men do courting their lady love. No sentimental gestures from me. She's mine and knows it. I smile broadly as we defy death and make our way to the island on the horizon.

Sounds like she's a short-heeled lass who fell under my marriage rod as well. No awkward first quiffing where I pretend to be sweet and loving. She knows my proclivities and still claims me. I just hope she wasn't part of the orgies…or one of the fireships that made the inside of my britches itch. My lips clench shut before my booze-loosened tongue can ask her if

Kraken can contract the pox, crabs, or heaven forbid—the Bube.

"I'm releasing you, so don't be difficult. Climb onto the beach and stay out of trouble while I rest. If you drown yourself after I carried you for miles, I'll haunt you in hell," she scolds between gulps of air.

Her tentacles release me in a teasing caress that awakens my senses. Nothing is sexier than the way she crawls up the beach with her ruby tentacles rippling behind her. My path isn't straight, and my strides are uneven, but I try my best to exit the ocean with a captain's swagger. She collapses before she reaches the edge. Her cheek rests on the sand as rain patters in a halo around her. I scoop her into my arms—tentacles flopping over my elbow—and arrange her on my lap. Watching the storm against the safety of a boulder, I can reflect on the miracle in my arms.

She's here. My lady love has found me. She resents how we met, but we can work on resolving our misunderstanding. However I treated her at our first passing, it wasn't with the respect she deserves. Our paths crossed too soon, and we've been given a second chance. We can build a future on the sea. I've never aspired to retire as a farmer or island merchant like most of me hearties. Landlubbing domestication sounds like soul-sucking wretchedness. This little lady proves my destiny is naval excitement with a bite of danger until my bitter end.

We doze on and off as the ocean's roar quiets to civil complaints. I dream of tentacles, and for the first time, I'm not frightened. I understand the octopus tarot card wasn't an heiress but a Kraken…my Kraken. My fingers tangle in her thick, red hair and stroke her cheek as she sleeps. Her breath warms my flesh between my shirt buttons. I wish I were topless too, so I could feel my lady love—skin to skin.

"You're awake," she whispers before rubbing her face on my chest. Her tiny fists grind into her eyes as she rubs the sleep from them.

"The sunrise woke me," I say in a voice rough with sleep. "The sweet trade trained me to sleep in short bursts."

"Short bursts when the sun's down?"

"Short bursts when Captain says so," I say with a chuckle. I'm dazzled by her smile when she laughs with me. My lady love is stunning.

"Well, you're Captain now," she says, patting my chest. She sits up, leaving a cold spot in her absence. "You need to retrieve your boat."

"We—" I stop when she places her hand over my mouth.

"There's no 'we' that you have to acknowledge. I didn't save you to earn your love or respect. The bond between us couldn't allow me to watch you die." She fiddles with a…scale?... belly button?... something at her waist, where she transitions from lady to octopus. "I must return to the sea before someone sees me, and I think you know the way to Maude's tavern from here."

"If you think I'm letting you slip away that easily, you buss my cheeks." I grab her elbow to haul her into my arms but release her when she flinches. She's not kidding. Will she allow some slight I don't remember to keep us apart?

"Seriously, Teeth, I feel eyes on me. Someone watches us. It's not safe for me to be on land in this form," she says as her tentacles reach for the water.

"I don't know your name! How will I find you?" Desperation pulls my heart into my throat. I've had two sober minutes with my lady love after a lifetime of searching. My ribs squeeze my stomach, and all the ocean water I swallowed gurgles in my belly.

"Our night together," she says with a world of hurt in her eyes, "you called me 'love.' I liked it, so why change now?"

I called her 'love' because that's what I call every whore I bed. All women swoon over it—making it easier for me to play under their skirts. The nickname keeps me from learning their names and allowing the guilt to chase me out to sea when I leave them behind. Promises of my return—which I never intended to keep—are easier to fabricate when they are nameless doxies and not people.

Shame lowers my chin. What have I done? Is this my punishment? Isn't losing my sister Melanie to brothel life punishment enough? I never hurt or stiffed a working girl. If she said 'no,' I moved on—but who am I kidding? By the time I asked her rates, most working girls would sweeten my sugarstick for free.

"Teeth," my lady calls from the sea. She's waded into the water up to her hips as I've wallowed in my past. "Tell Maude that Sabrina sent you. She'll assign a girl to take care of you."

Chapter 7

Sabrina

"Stop."

One word.

If he yelled like a petulant child, I could ignore him, but his quiet authority freezes me in place. With each step of his approach, my tentacles ball tighter beneath me. I shrink as he grows larger than life. Arguments die on my tongue. I should check for fishermen heading out at first light, but I can't take my eyes off Teeth.

The breeze ruffles his hair, lifting tendrils around his face like seaweed dancing underwater. The muscles across his chest and over his shoulders bunch and release beneath his damp linen shirt. I can imagine him as a Kraken under the ocean. His torso is steady, as if he glides on tentacles, but the splashes of his boots kicking the water ruin the illusion.

My eyes roam down his body—to check for tentacles, yeah, right—and find the bulge in his leathers. He wants me, but more surprising is how much I want him. I hate the heat building in me as he nears. Whether it is spiteful or lustful passion, I can't control my response to him. We could never go back to strangers in a tavern. A force would pull us together from across the barroom floor.

"I'm not done with you." He stops just short of his body heat reaching me. The water swirls around his hips, so I get an enticing peek at my prize with each retreat of the tide, only to have it taken away by the next wave. His thumb and forefinger lift my chin. He doesn't touch me anywhere else.

"Please." I don't know if I'm asking him to let me leave or to gather me into his embrace. Every second my Kraken form is possibly exposed to prying eyes is a threat to my life, and every second I spend with him is a threat to my heart.

"I intend to please you," he says with a lazy half-smile.

I know he can. We both do. I burn everywhere he touched me in my human form all those years ago. My soulbeak tingles. The damn thing better stay in place and not sacrifice my life to his care. I'm not wearing clothes to contain it. What if he ingests my soulbeak—without understanding the commitment it initiates? He will choose his crew, piracy, and life as a human for both of us. I'll be trapped on two legs roaming the earth in loneliness as one of his hearties. Or worse, he will sail away while I join Maude's working girls to survive.

My lips tremble with unspoken protests as he draws me into his arms. His kiss is as hard and demanding as he is. I yield despite the warning bells clamoring in my head. My mouth opens before he can force his way in. It's inevitable. He will own me. I slide my front tentacles up his legs in possessive coils. Devil may have me, but I can't resist his offer. A third tentacle loops around the hand he rests at his side to guide it to my breast.

We aren't friends or even acquaintances. I don't know his favorite foods, memories, or friends. He likes piracy, drinking liquor, and whores. *What a winner.* However, from a safe distance in the sea, I've watched him coach his junior crew members, learn to read, and sail the boat at every position—from ratlines as a sailor to the helm as captain. Isn't bettering oneself the biggest achievement of all? Could Captain Teeth be a mature version of Sailor Teeth, who abandoned me? Do I dare trust my intuition that says our paths crossed now because he's ready to settle down?

"Climb up, Sabs," he commands against my lips. His hand leaves my chin to untie his britches. "Take your pleasure and teach me how to quiff a Kraken."

My name on his lips steals the breath from my

lungs, but the risk is too big.

"I can't be another conquest. Not here—"

"This might sound strange, but I believe you when you call me your mate. I went to a fortune teller whose cards said the octopus card represented my lady love. Chub—smartest hearty on the boat—said the octopus was an ace of diamonds and you'd be a rich lass. But here you are…half octopus. I'm not asking to conquer *a Kraken*. I'm asking *my future wife* to give me a banging farewell before she swims off to find my damn boat."

"We don't know each other. Mates are the way of Kraken but not humans—"

"I've sailed with magic bowls, a woman who weaves like a spider, a Hoodoo priestess, a vampiress…I have met the devil himself in Blackbeard. I lost my ties to humanity and prejudices against *others* long ago. I don't question the mystical nature of our courtship, and neither should you, Sabs."

Future wife. Sabs, a nickname. Courtship. Belonging. Damn him, I want them all.

My front tentacles glide up the hard planes of his body to wrap around his neck. They coil around one another to give me an anchor. I raise my weight out of the water until his tip pokes at my siphon's pouch—inches from my soulbeak on my belly. The errant scale burns like the fires of hell. With two tentacles on the sandy bottom, two wrapped around his legs, and two squeezing my breasts as he watches with burning intensity, I position myself to join us.

"Will you bend so I can stick you between the tentacles?" His words come out like a marlin who escaped a Kraken's grasp.

"You want your cock in my beaked mouth? You trust me not to snap it off with my beak and razor-sharp teeth?" I tease him because the terrified look on his face is priceless. I wrap my hands around his cock to intensify the threat. "How about I take you in my siphon slit where it's warm, wet, and produces unbelievable suction?"

"Show me." He's bewildered but excited. His eyes dart up and down my body as if presented with a meal he doesn't know how to devour.

My tentacles move his hands to my nipples again to coax his fingers to roll them how I like best. As he busies himself pleasing me, I breathe open my siphon's pouch just above my pelvic bone. Saltwater rushes in. The chill zaps my feverish insides. My siphon muscles contract to squirt it out but freeze when he groans. Oops, the heated water blasted his cock. He bites his bottom lip with his chin tilted toward the sky.

"Stop teasing me," he moans.

I guide his tip into my siphon and tighten the tentacles around his neck to push him inside to the hilt.

A pelican flying overhead would make the same strangled squawk as Teeth. My siphon muscles contract and release in rhythmic pulses to mimic my swimming across the ocean. The intensity can propel my body almost a mile…or suck my mate's cock harder than any human's mouth. Any other man, I'd worry about injury, but my *experienced* mate has desensitized himself for me.

Proof we are physically a perfect match.

My tentacles on the ocean floor wrap around his ankles to replace the ones climbing his legs and into his britches. His hands learn my body with tender caresses as I hold myself in his care. Our kisses are slow swipes and gentle nips at one another's lips as if we have a lifetime to demonstrate our love for one another. The reality that we are strangers drifts away on the morning tide. The suckers on my tentacles flare open to taste every inch of him.

The destined bond between us sings in my heart as joy floods my veins. A tentacle slithers to the apex of his thighs to writhe against his nutmegs and nudge his windward passage with each sway of our bodies. Ink swirls around us in the water as my thrusts accelerate. He groans in my mouth as I penetrate him, locking us together in an infinite loop. Pleasure blooms along the edges of my siphon pouch as they plump with arousal. We're so close, I'm lost as to where I end and he begins. I'm overwhelmed with a sense of my fate aligning with his.

"Peak for me, Sabs," he whispers. He bites my ear. I see stars as my body lets go. My tentacles mimic the pulsing of my siphon. I bury my face in his chest to muffle my cries of rapture. He floods my body with his release, triggering another storm inside me. Tears gather at the corners of my eyes as I fight my mind for control. Sensations zip through my body with alarming speed, so I'm bombarded by pleasure from head to tentacle tip.

"Kinky minx," he whispers with a grunt as I withdraw my tentacle from him. "If I didn't believe your prophecy before, I do now."

"Does that mean you will take the time to get to know me?" I hate how needy I sound, but my soulbeak has more power over my mouth than my air-starved brain.

"I won't rest until we find a way to be together," he whispers against my lips. His hands tangle in my hair as our kiss deepens.

The stirrings of love within me churn like stormy seas. I wish I could stay in this moment forever, but the burning of someone watching me returns with the rush of blood back to my head. I must flee to the depths where humans won't go. The Caribbean is a small place for a Kraken, and I have found his boat repeatedly over the years. I will find him again. Self-preservation finally overpowers my soulbond, and I lower my tentacles into the cold ocean.

"Then I'm confident in leaving you for now. I'll look for *Patricia's Wish* on the seas while you look in the harbor. If you find her first, set sail, so we can meet again."

"Stay in my arms for a few more minutes—"

"The sun is high in the sky. Someone will see me," I say with a whimper.

"I can protect you. I'll slice them to ribbons." By the fates, I believe him. Even if his fervent promises are just for today, he means the sweet words. It's in the reverent way he lowers me into the water. My tentacles spread out on the seafloor to cool themselves. He pets my hair as I lean against his thigh.

Why do my insides cry? Is this tryst different from the last one? He may wipe my feelings from his memory like the first time I fell for him. I've been more honest with who I am and my intentions, but has he? We crashed together like sea animals in a mating frenzy, but is that enough to tempt him to get to know me?

"Go on, Sabs," he says quietly. "Swim off so I know you're safe."

"You walk away first," I reply. "I'll hear anyone approaching in the water."

"You're the one who is worried that we're being watched. I've always fancied myself an erotic showman—"

"Don't make promises you can't keep."

"I could fall in love with you, you know," he says before bending over to capture my lips one last time. He stomps through the surf, lacing his pants as he returns to land. Strands of his hair dance around his head in a chaotic halo. The sand beneath his boots crunches as if greeting him as underlings. His glance over his shoulder and soft, half smile melt my heart. It isn't the farewell smirk of a conquest, but the shy grin of someone in a new relationship.

I sink under the water to wet my hair. If he looks back again, his last glimpse of me won't be as frightening. I finger-comb the locks the best I can. When I emerge once more, he's vanished—presumably to the opposite side of the boulders. It's just as well. The sooner we part, the sooner we will reunite. The next time he talks to his lady love over the side of the boat, I'll answer. He won't pour liquor into the sea; he'll lick it off my tentacle's suckers.

In two weeks, I'll have legs again. Maybe he will give me a tour of his boat and introduce me to his crew…as his lady love. Maybe we will wed. He's talked about his anxieties over marrying his quartermaster to his cook. Would marrying me make him nervous too? After I explain my soulbeak, he won't have reason to be. He has part-time freedom unless he takes it. The future and power in our relationship is in his hands...like it always has been.

Maybe nothing has changed after all.

Ouch!

A net falls over me, tangling in my tentacles. A second net crisscrosses over the first. I unsheathe my knife and saw at the ropes of the first net. Why didn't I take my knife to be sharpened two weeks ago when I was last human? The dull blade wastes valuable seconds gliding over the strands instead of cutting through them. I give up on cutting my way out.

I lean toward the deep. My tentacles dig into the sand as far out as I can reach. They bend to drag my body...and the bodies on the other end of the ropes...into the ocean. Curses and whistles beckon me to stare down my attackers, but I must focus on returning to the ocean. If I stop pulling with all my might for even a second, they will yank the closing cords on the nets and drag my tentacles from the sand. I'll seal my doom. Pull. *Pull.*

"Gotcha now," says a masculine voice. Two black, beady eyes lock with mine before a sharp-smelling rag is forced over my nose and mouth.

"Gills, you bastard," I shout from behind the rag. As long as my gills are submerged, I can bring rich seawater through my vocal cords to speak. Each exhale soaks the rag and dilutes the foul liquid on it. "You can't poison me this way."

"Only I'm not alone," he says with an evil laugh. A group of men gather around me, holding the ropes to the net. They dislodge my tentacles from the sand. I struggle, but each man wrestles a tentacle. There are too many of them. They lift my body from the water. I hold my breath as I twist and writhe to escape their punishing grip.

After minutes, I'm forced to inhale, and everything goes black.

Chapter

8

Captain Teeth

"Ahoy! It's Cap'n Teeth!" Eze shouts from the second-story window of Maude's Tavern as I approach.

Rochelle, Cami, and Esmerelda stick their heads out the window to whistle and call me. Yesterday, I'd have welcomed their attention to lift my spirits. Today, I'm bound to a Kraken—a Kraken who would crack my nutmegs with her tentacles if she found me between their legs. I reach for my hat to wave to the youngster and his purchased bedfellows, only to come away empty-handed. Some lucky sod in Davy Jones's locker has a new, feather-lined hat.

"I knew the sea would spit you out eventually," Chub says from the doorway. The half doors of the tavern are eye-level with me hearty, but the way he fills the threshold says volumes about his strength. His arm wraps around Catalina's hips, bunching her silk-spun dress up her thighs. She's as scantily dressed as the doxies but by choice instead of profession. She could be collecting gold for her lacy frocks but chooses to weave ropes for us.

"I was too much for the old girl," I reply with a wink.

"More like the sea didn't like the taste of whatever grows in your leathers," he retorts with a loud guffaw.

"She didn't complain," I say with a smug smile that has me hearty pausing. I take his bacon face between my palms and stare into his blue eyes. "I met her Chub. When I fell into the drink last night, I met my lady love."

"I wondered what happened to you. A captain never leaves his ship, especially a quality man like yourself. You scared me, matey."

"You scared all of us," Catalina adds. She takes my hand in both of hers and leads me to the first long table.

Greenhorn scrambles to vacate the end of the bench until I lean on his shoulder to stay. Plopping down beside him, I sample the drink Catalina thrusts into my hand. The table digs into my back as I lean my elbows on it, but the pain is good. It reminds me I'm alive and awake—Sabs's rescue wasn't a dream. Chub climbs onto the bench on my other side and pulls Catalina onto his thigh. Her tiny feet kick my knees as she swings her legs over Chub's lap. Just wait until Chub is hit by Sabs's tentacles when I cuddle her!

"So, your drunk arse fell into the drink," Chub starts with a wry smile twisting his lips.

"I would have drowned if not for Sabs—Sabrina. My lady love's name is Sabrina," I blurt out, the excitement in my heart pouring into the room. "She's everything I hoped for and more.

"She a mermaid? Or a siren?" Greenhorn asks, barely containing his laughter. Yeah, when I was a whippersnapper, I would have laughed at my current state, too. There was a time when yoking myself to one woman was my worst nightmare.

"Worse," I sneer. He cowers as he remembers I'm not just his hearty at a bar; I'm his captain who has the right to maroon his arse on this island if I see fit. If he wants a spot on *Patricia's Wish* when we leave port, he shouldn't cross me. "She's a Kraken most days. She says she's human on the full moon. That's how I met her before—we rode the St. George one night under this very roof."

"A Kraken bussie, I'll be damned," Chub says, saluting me with his tankard of rum.

"Sharp-tongued and strong as an ox, too. She dragged me to the beach in last night's storm—cursing and bitching at me the whole way. I've never met such a fiery temper in a woman—"

"You best not be talking about one of my girls, Teeth. I won't have you blaming your itchy sugarstick on my working girls when we both know you could have caught the Bube anywhere in the Caribbean!" Maude's tired dress with the faded toucan has seen better days. Her hair still reaches the sky, but half the curls wrapped in the bandana are grey.

The ruby lips that have scolded me since I first docked on Trinidad with Ol'Blackbeard have thinned to a slash across her stern face. I remember how her eyes would twinkle with the potential earnings from stupid, young bucks like me jumping from the ratlines and into her whore's straw beds. Now, I'm the Crusty Captain who watches my crew ascend her stairs with memories flashing before my eyes. At one point, I climbed those stairs with Sabrina—too stupid to realize what I had in my hands.

Never again.

"Do you remember a redhead named Sabrina?"

"Oh, that girl," Maude says with a roll of her coal-rimmed eyes. "She's as scandalous as you. You'd be best to keep away from that troublemaker! She only comes around on the full moon like some bat out of hell and stirs up the men into a frenzy."

"How so?" Catalina asks with eyes wide with concern.

"Sometimes she beds the whole bar—two or

three at a time. Other times, she won't touch a soul and sleeps alone upstairs. Men love a fickle woman because the chase is half the fun."

"Was she on the payroll?" Chub asks with his drink casually lifting to his mouth. He's testing Maude, but to what end? To see if she would keep us apart? To learn more about Sabs? I wish I could pull him aside and ask where his mind has sailed his questions.

"She knew the business because she tipped out to me each morning," Maude says with a shrug. Chub taps the table with his marriage finger. I see! Maude curls her fingers into fists. She's not so indifferent to Sabrina's antics. "She always paid for her room, unlike a girl on my payroll—I take care of my girls—and tipped the barmen handsomely. Sometimes the moon would rise, and she wouldn't show up. Then the real trouble would start. Sailors from rival boats would blame one another for scaring her off or hoarding her under their decks. She's more trouble than she's worth if you ask me."

"Yet you never turned her away," Catalina says with a cold undercurrent that has Chub holding her closer.

"Money is money," Maude says, returning to her jovial facade. "I took what I could from her while I could. I doubt I'll see her again."

"Because she will be married soon," I say with

pride, puffing out my chest.

"Oh no," Maude says with an ominous shake of her head. "Because those scouts from the mainland came looking for her."

"Scouts?"

"They hunt for talent to work their shows on the continent, but once a year, they host performances on the islands. They need girls to lift the curtains from their acts and sell tobacco in the crowds. It's a bonus if the girl can sing or dance—and Sabrina can do both. I wouldn't be surprised if she's in the island's show this month. When they leave for the next island and eventually sail to the continent, she will travel with them."

"Does that worry you? Are the men kind?"

"I worry about all my girls," Maude says as she squints fake tears to the corners of her eyes. "The girls who go into the shows never return, and I'm overjoyed for them. They get a new start, in a new town, as showgirls instead of whores. They meet husbands and settle down—I just know it."

"That's not what will happen to Sabs," I growl. "We have an understanding."

"Do you, now? Oh Teeth, half the men who drink at these tables think they have an understanding with Sabrina. Don't be a fool," she scolds.

My insecurities wash over me like a tidal wave.

Walk the Walk

Book 5: Hooking Captain Teeth

All the years of hiding my uneducated mind behind Chub's schemes and my pretty face come back to haunt me like ghosts long drowned in my psyche. I can read, but only with me hearty's lessons in the past year. My missing fingers aren't why I can't write more than my signature. I never learned. I spent my youth begging for food and dodging brothels that pedaled young boys. My years on the ratlines alternated between blowing my earnings and pirate raids instead of apprenticing under learned sailors and bettering myself.

If only I had followed Chub's lead instead of laughing at him. Would I know if Sabrina was pulling one over on me?

You can't fake having tentacles…but what if I wanted the fortune teller's prophecy to be true so badly that I fell for the first tentacled lady I met? I mean…how many tentacled ladies does a man meet in a lifetime? Any sane pirate would say zero, but I'm the captain of *Patricia's Wish,* where we seem to attract women who are *other*. Does that include Sabrina?

"By order of King George the First—stay where you are!" Shouts a voice from the doorway.

"You can't burst in here and tell my patrons what to do!" Maude leaves our table to bump chests with the trio of English soldiers in her doorway. "You can take your war outside! I don't care who owns this island—

Walk the Walk

Book 5: Hooking Captain Teeth

Spain or England—in this tavern, it doesn't change a thing. I've owned this business since you were a babe sucking your mother's tit and will continue operations long after your daughters become my working girls!"

"Leave my daughters out of this," sneers the soldier closest to her.

"Then leave the building because I think I recognize you. I employ a whore with a nose just like yours—"

The crack of his backhand across Maude's face echoes throughout the tavern.

Nobody moves.

Silence descends on the tavern as everyone gawks at Maude's fall to the floor. She rubs her cheek as she stands, pats her hair, and straightens the threadbare shawl around her shoulders. Like a queen, she turns her back on the soldiers and addresses the bar with her chin held high…but tears flow down her face.

"Whoever brings me this soldier's head gets free drinks for life," she declares.

The ring of Chub's machete as he unsheathes it behind Catalina's back is the signal of authority I need.

"You heard her, mateys! Who's thirsty?" My shouts are met with a chorus of cheers from me hearties. I jump to my feet and thrust my longsword in the air with a roar. In seconds, I'm surrounded by bloodthirsty pirates, the chronically arrested, and day-drunk patrons spoiling for a fight. We crash the entrance with the business end of our swords leading the way.

The leather binding Catalina's wrists flutters to the ground as she unleashes her spinnerets. Ten strands of spider's thread fly across the bar's entrance and wrap around Maude's arms. Chub grabs his spider lady's hands, and the pair tug Maude out of the fray. He tucks the ladies behind him before joining me on my left flank—the designated place for a quartermaster.

This is why I'd never survive the life of a landlubber. I'd pick fights with these mollies for amusement every day. The trio uses practiced moves from their academies with fancy footwork and designated pauses between each coordinated sequence. They puff to twice their size when six more soldiers and the street police join them. I'd bend over and laugh my arse off if they wouldn't stab me in the back.

The soldier who assaulted Maude points a short gun at my face. With a shouted order, the soldiers in front of him duck…but so do the pirates they have engaged in combat. We meet eyes. The barrel waves as the tremors in his hands give away his fear. I stand my ground and glare at him, daring him to shoot me in cold blood. He fires. I hit the deck before the smoke clears. With my belly collecting dust from the dirty floor, I watch his shiny boots exit the tavern and clack down the cobblestone street.

Lilly-livered Molly.

Raising to my feet, I'm instantly engaged in swordplay against two enemies. I slash the largest soldier across the belly when he lifts his sword over his head. His free hand covers the wound as his sword comes down with half the strength required. I bat it away like a mosquito and tsk at him. He doubles over to look at the damage to his waistline as if he believes I'll pause the battle for him. Does he think he's in a training yard and I'm a fellow student? I can't resist. The handle of my sword slams into the back of his head, and he drops like a sack of potatoes.

I raise an eyebrow at his partner. The man is frozen until I wiggle my fingers at him. He swings his sword with his left hand in a broad arc. I lazily step out of the way and sucker punch him in the grogblossom. Blood sprays from his left nostril, combining with the tracks of tears down his cheeks. He drops his sword to cup his hands over his face. A strange wheezing noise reverberates from behind his fingers before he bends over to catch his breath. I slam the hilt of my sword onto the top of his head to drop him next to his partner.

I find no joy in stabbing them through the heart…the fight was over too soon.

Where have all the competent soldiers gone?

Walk the Walk

Book 5: Hooking Captain Teeth

"Captain," shrieks Greenhorn, my newest addition to my crew. He slashes and thrashes his short sword at a soldier who hasn't broken a sweat. If the soldier would break his choreographed steps and actually fight, Greenhorn would be a filling for a pine box.

"For all that's holy, watch his movements! He's repeating the same bloody steps," I grouse as I step over my former opponent. I stomp with Chub at my heels to where Greenhorn has frozen. His sword is fast enough to block the soldier's thrusts and jabs without all the fancy footwork.

"Jab left, jab left, right thrust, parlay back," Greenhorn sings as if the soldier can't hear him. "You're right! This nutmeg is stuck in his head as if he's swirling down a whirlpool."

"I'll kill you, scoundrel," his opponent yells. "We will clean the streets of pirating scum like you and claim this island in the name of King—"

"Oh, save it!" Chub yells as he slashes the soldier across the throat. "I have no patience for royal rhetoric without booze!"

"You saved the tavern! How can I ever repay you?" Maude's sour milk smell fills my nose as she presses against me.

"Looks like one of you land lubbers will earn Maude's free drinks. The yellow-bellied sod who hit

Maude went rogue. Remember her promise and bring her his head!" I yell to the crowd, who raise their weapons and cheer. "Me hearties' work here is done. Let's weigh anchor! We've got a Kraken to hunt!"

"A Kraken? Did it threaten your boat? Is it dangerous?" Maude asks, fluttering her eyelashes.

"Not to you—" I remove her hand from my chest and glide a few inches away from her "—but she will be the death of my patronage to your working girls. The next time you see me, I'll be a married man."

Chapter

9

Sabrina

"We've fired the irons, so don't give us any trouble," grumbles my burly handler. The burns on my arms, back, and tentacles itch at the sound of his voice. Little round buttons of torture dot my body, reminders of the times I had the energy to fight. Between living in my own excrement and cramped conditions for my tentacles, my body is too sick to lash out at my captors.

He lifts the lid off the watertight barrel that has been my home for the last two weeks. I'm blinded by the early evening sun after sitting in complete darkness for hours. Despite the filthy water's rancid taste, I cower deeper into the oversized barrel. He grabs me by the shoulders to drag me from my prison. I hit the floor on my elbow and cry out from the impact. My tentacles slither from the barrel to coil around me like armor.

"Shut up," he yells as he kicks me in the back.

I cough and sob as the agony races up my spine. What I wouldn't do for an hour in the sea?! I'd stretch

Walk the Walk

Book 5: Hooking Captain Teeth

my tentacles along the warm sand of the bottom, cleanse my gills, feed on fresh fish, and never take my freedom for granted again. My daydream takes my consciousness away as I'm groped and manhandled by the show's stagehands. Weights are chained to my tentacles to slow me down. My wrists are bound to my neck in an elaborate, beaded harness connected to a leather leash. I hold onto my vision of the open water—that way, I don't think about who this harness was originally made for or what became of her.

"Never thought I'd see the day she'd submit," says Ol'Barnabie with a belly laugh. He crouches so his cigar dangles an inch from the end of my nose. "This fish was a maneater who took on six men with whaling nets. Now she's my little doll who lets me pull her strings in any fashion I want."

His evil laughter chills me to the bone.

"You stay sweet until after showtime, and I may have Rufus and Dolbie put new saltwater in your tank. Would you like that? Have you had enough of swimming in my piss, or have you enjoyed adding your own?" When I drop my chin to cry, he kisses my forehead. The slimy imprint of his lips is worse than the burnt brands from the irons.

Thankfully, Rufus throws a bucket of cold seawater over my head. If I had a warning, I would have opened my gills to clean them. Outside the barrel,

Walk the Walk

Book 5: Hooking Captain Teeth

I use my lungs to breathe, but inside, my gills must filter air from the piss-soaked water. My head is jerked backward as one of the men pulls my hair off my shoulders. Their dirty hands wring gray water from the strands. Satisfied I won't drip on the stage where Barnabie would slip, they tuck the mass into my collar.

"Can't let the fringe cover what the audience is here to see—the menfolk, at least. Our profits rose by two since we added you to our freak show," Rufus laughs. The joke's on him. The venue doubles in size with each island we visit. I bet Barnabie is raking in doubloons hand over fist but tells these nutmegs the revenue raises slightly to keep the excess.

"Yeah," Dolbie chimes in. "I bet the boss could do better if he allowed the punters to pet her dairy. Then we would be rolling in coins."

"Nah," Rufus says with a yank on my leash to follow him. "We're not that type of show—that would anger the local madams who help us fence the authorities."

"The authorities are in the audience!"

"On the islands, yeah, but on the continent? No way would those Puritan scoundrels be caught dead at a show with dairy exposed. Half the wenches aren't allowed to show their shoulders or ankles. A breast might send the preachers to the golden gates early."

Lifting each weighted tentacle is a struggle. I

must concentrate to get one weight off the ground. My palms slap the ground as I crawl when I normally glide upright. The beaded chains on my chest scrape the dirt, and a dust cloud tickles my nose. Still, my handlers pull my leash, angling my neck so my chin touches my collarbone. Black spots wink in my vision as my air is cut off. My gills moan and wheeze as they compensate for my lung's lack of air.

"Let's go," Rufus whispers tersely before grabbing my two front tentacles. Their weights dangle from his arms. Their cuffs cut into my flesh. Blood beads where tentacle meets metal.

"He's telling the story of how she capsized his ship and he wrestled her to shore, so it will be a tick before she's needed," Dolbie says while picking up my back two tentacles. He's mindful to scoop up the weights as well.

With half the tentacles' weights to move, I use every ounce of strength to slither across the floor. I'm grateful Rufus and Dolbie carry my fore and aft tentacles instead of pushing me forward with the branding iron—although my position above the ground makes me walk on tentacle tips like tiptoes—I'm swiftly transferred from the show's creature wagon to my show tank. The bearded lady, the lizard boy, and the cyclops nod their heads in respect as I pass. I hear their conversations at night, but none dare to speak to the monster in the barrel. After my arrival, their time in the show was cut. Less work and better conditions make me a hero in their eyes—even if they are terrified of me.

I'm glad someone is because I feel myself slipping away.

The fantasies of Captain Teeth and his demon pirate crew rescuing me kept me alive and fighting the first few days. For several days following that, I fought out of rage against the branding irons. Now, I hope for the end. I have two more days until the full moon. Maybe I'll be lucky and suffocate in my piss barrel. As much as I wish I could take out these vile men and save Bettina from ever meeting them, I don't have it in me to save myself.

Not anymore.

With the grunts and grabby hands, Rufus and Dolbie dump me into my show tank. I dodge my chains and the weights on my tentacles as they are carelessly thrown in after me and sink to the bottom. *Ahhh,* fresh water. It's not saltwater, but it's clear enough for the customers to gawk at me through the glass on the front of the enclosure, so it's free of feces. I scrub my scalp to coax my hair from my collar and shake away debris. My precious moments of sunlight end as a tarp is thrown over the tank. The wooden wheels squeak and groan as I'm transferred to the stage.

"And here's the she-devil! The Beast of the Caribbean! The Kraken who sunk my boat, ate my crew, but was no match for me—"

I roll my eyes at Barnabie's blustering. One look at his shiny boots would tell anyone he's never worked a deck a minute of his life. *As if I had the appetite to eat a crew of men? No wonder the rotund, balding man could catch me! I'd be stuffed to the gills and too sick to fight back. Ha!* Barnabie's act would become a comedy if this tank didn't stifle my sarcasm. If the glass were thinner or metal reinforcements didn't adorn the seams, I could throw one-liners from under the tarp to punch holes in his ludicrous story.

The crowd gasps when the tarp is removed. They always do. Men lean forward and adjust their spectacles to sneak a glimpse of my naked breasts before their wives catch on. Some children point while others hide in their mother's skirts.

They aren't the worst. The worst are the women in the crowd. Furious at their men, most of them want to butcher me and serve me on their kitchen table—according to what they yell at my tank. But I suffer worse abuse than words at small shows. Will Barnabie grip my hair, pulling against the tentacle weights, so my human half hangs limply over my tank in a display of his dominance? At least the women don't give him the admiration he seeks. Small justice. The ladies cover their noses with handkerchiefs at my smell. Lower-class women throw rotten produce at me.

He's ignored...so he books increasingly larger crowds... Based on the size of this audience, he will keep me enclosed. He's packed the tent to the rafters. I scan the frightened faces as Barnabie's tale drones on...

Wait?! Could it be? It is!

In the far reaches of the crowd sit a dust-coated bunch of children. Unlike the rest of the children in attendance, these sit still with wide eyes ringed with the black shadows of poverty. Like the shining beacon of a lighthouse, Bettina's preacher's stove pipe hat calls to me. I swim to the opposite side of the tank and press myself against the enclosure seam. Ignoring the hisses and squeals of the front row, I scan the sea of urchins for my sister.

She waves her gloved fingers. Her jaw rests on the high-neck collar of her dress.

Yeah, I know. Shocker. Now get me out.

We stare at one another until Barnabie finishes his story. The audience is invited to roam the space and get close to his creatures. I was tonight's finale, but the cat man, the four-armed lady, and the mermaid—who I suspect is a manatee in makeup—are also in tanks around the room. Some nights, I flash my breasts at the snobby women who approach my tank. Other nights, I ball my tentacles and sulk until Barnabie pokes me with a hot iron in front of everyone. Those nights are the worst because none of the people bat an eyelash at the abuse.

Bettina will care. She'll scream at him until he loses his hearing in one ear.

As my sister rushes to my tank, I'm smacked by the realization that she's on legs. How is she in human form? The full moon is in two days. How is she walking? While the crowd gapes at me, I gawk at her plain linen dress. She places her gloves flat against the glass, and I press my palms to my side. Her eyes fill with tears. I shake my head at her that this isn't the time for a rescue. More than Rufus and Dolbie, Barnabie bribes the port authorities to act as security guards during the shows. Even in Kraken form, she wouldn't stand a chance.

"Almost makes you believe she's a woman," Pastor Richard whispers.

His breath fogs the glass. Wide eyes roam over my body. I drop my connection with Bettina to fold my arms and tuck my hands in my armpits to shield my breasts. In all the years I've swum nude under the sea and stripped to my human skin in bawdy taverns, I've never felt as dirty as under his stare. My skin crawls where his gaze lands. Bettina squints at him as if she's about to unleash one of her purity tirades when

Barnabie's shadow darkens their shoulders.

"Want to pet her, Pastor?" The slimy showman worms his way between Bettina and her date. She trips over the hem of her dress as she backs away, but Barnabie's arm snakes around her middle to catch her. I don't miss the way his fingers press into her breast under her arm. Bettina gasps but otherwise doesn't give into her Kraken instinct to rip into the man.

"Oh no, she's an abomination," Richard states indignantly as if he wasn't salivating over my curves a second ago. "A soulless monster like her should be put down. Sending this demon back to hell, instead of tempting my parishioners to touch her flesh, would be the righteous thing to do."

"How do you know she's a demon?" Bettina asks from under Barnabie's arm. Her eyebrows wiggle at Richard to rescue her from the groping showman, but he ignores her plight. "Just because her body is different doesn't mean her heart can't be pure."

"I can assure you," Barnabie says, leaning to peek inside my sister's dress. *Ha!* Bettina's neckline doesn't give away a freckle under her chin, let alone a glimpse of cleavage. "Her body is identical to a woman's—tentacles aside—and I invite you to feel for yourself."

"Well, I never," Bettina says with her hand over her heart.

"That's quite enough," Richard declares. Just when I thought he'd forgotten them completely, he grabs the hands of the two closest children. Great idea—bring impressionable kids to a show that goes against your teachings. What was he thinking? "The island's residents will hear the Lord's opinion on your show. I would never return to Trinidad if I were a businessman like yourself. Your seats will undoubtedly be empty! Come along, children, we must repent for what we have seen."

I wave goodbye to Bettina while Barnabie's back is turned. She's my last hope, but her pastor will never let her help me now. If she's on legs, she gave him her soulbeak, and he chose for them to live as humans. Based on his attitude toward me, I doubt she told him our Kraken lifestyle was an option. She's in love and living happily ever after, surrounded by children. I can't ruin her life. At least she won't wonder what happened to me.

I won't live past the full moon.

"He can be quite feisty," Bettina says to Barnabie, but loud enough that I believe her message is to me. "Is there anything I can do to help?"

Barnabie launches into his usual threats about how the port authorities side with him and how his following on the continent makes touring the islands not worth the hassle. As he drones on about how his visits are acts of charity, Bettina stares at me over his shoulder.

I point to my teeth.

For the first time since I last saw her in her Kraken form, my sister smiles.

Help is on the way, but will he reach me before my human form drowns?

Chapter 10

Captain Teeth

"Eze pull the gangplank. Master of Sails, are we ready to weigh anchor?" I shout the final orders to leave Trinidad's harbor. By now, half the boats docked on their pier have spotted the Spanish Galleon on the horizon, but *Patricia's Wish* can outrun them all. Instead of a massive slaver's vessel, like the *Whydah*, our girl is an English man-o-war we stole in Carolina. She's faster, sleeker, and turns on a needle. We will engage with the Galleon first and, by the law of the sea, be the ones to plunder her. Whether or not the Galleon has treasure, she will fill our larder and armory.

Sometimes the best booty is found in the kitchen, not the cargo hold.

"Sails unfurled, Sir. Throw the lines, lads," Chub yells in response to my order. The pirates who untied the sails scramble onto the deck to untie the tow lines that hold us to the docks.

"Stop, stop," yells a daft wench from the

boardwalk. She holds her modest dress to her knees as she runs toward the boat.

I do a doubletake. She's the spitting image of my Sabs, but Sabs wouldn't wear a high collar like that—not when she claims I mistook her for a strumpet. This irritant's hair fans over her shoulders, where Sabs's hair hangs around her hips. It's the same color…is blazing red a common color in the Caribbean? What am I saying? Sabs wasn't raised in the masses of the Caribbean—she's a Kraken, so ask my arse if there's a redheaded island somewhere.

"Permission to board," she yells while stepping onto the gangplank.

The insolence!

"Permission denied," I shout to Eze, who obediently pulls the gangplank toward him. Irritating woman rides the gangplank as it's yanked aboard. She wobbles on worn shoes at odds with her fancy-collared dress. "We weigh anchor to engage the Spanish Galleon—not the place for a highborn lady."

"You can't leave," she shouts on the verge of hysterical sobs. Great, a delicate woman aboard is the last thing I need. She storms across the main deck and dares to approach me on the sterncastle deck. I have many female crewmembers who would kill a soldier to protect the boat—women I respect with my full heart—not like this delicate flower. "You must help me find my sister—"

"We must claim our prize, madam! Look around you," I sneer as I cross by Chub at the helm. "We aren't errand boys for the harbormaster. We're pirates!"

"If I help you claim this prize, will you return to Trinidad and help me rescue my sister?"

"No," I snarl. "Chub, full spin to the east. Master of Arms—is the crew equipped?"

"Aye, aye," shouts Barrel, who runs our armory. Blimey, a sword in every hand and a single shooter in every holster. Finally, someone who recognizes what must happen before they are told.

"Master of Cannons—"

"Four balls each and stocked with powder," yells the new gunnery we picked up in Aruba. What's his name? Did we rename him? Avast ye, I'll have to ask Chub when we're counting our spoils.

"Don't open the hatches until I give the order," I command. Chub gives me a wink and a nod in my peripheral vision. After months of studying, I finally learned Captain Magda, Captain Branko, and Ol'Blackbeard's maneuvers. If I have to spend another minute at the map with the little figures, I'll lose my temper and blow the models to smithereens. However, the toil will be worth it if our boat is in one piece after today's battle.

"Please—" Oh hell, is she still on deck? We're

at seventy yards and closing in. At twenty-five yards, I'll give the signal to turn and fire.

"You belong in the kitchen—"

"Well, I never—"

"The kitchen is where we have a false wall with a safe room for delicate people. Catalina will let you in and take care of you. Don't be difficult and go," I shout in her face. She squeezes her eyes shut as locks of red hair blow backward.

"If it's all the same to you," she says, smoothing her lacy collar against her neck. "I'll stay by your side. If you die, you can't retrieve my sister."

"Bloody hell," I reply, smearing my hand down my face. "If you stay by my side, crouch below the railing. I'm the target for their cannons, but your red hair makes you an easier mark."

Finally, the wench shows some sense and pales at my warning. With one last nod to Chub, I stomp across the deck to the front of the boat. My little shadow crouches lower than the railing as she shuffles behind me. I'll taunt the enemy from the forecastle deck by swinging out on the bowsprit to distract the snipers and cannoneers. Other boats sink when their captain is shot, but my quartermaster is the real brains behind this operation. *Patricia's Wish* will continue her attack as long as the enemy fire doesn't hit the helm he holds or the kitchen where his lady love resides.

Walk the Walk

Book 5: Hooking Captain Teeth

"Turn the sails south," I yell as my boots hit the forecastle stairs. The order repeats across the boat, called out by those on the deck as they tug the lines holding the sails and those on the ratlines as they kick the booms holding the fabric. The last to call the order is Chub, who tilts the wheel to turn the ship's rudder. The boat turns left and circles the Galleon like a shark.

"Are you going to ram her or fire at her?" The wench breaks my concentration with her nattering, repeating the same question until I'm compelled to answer her.

"Right now, we're stopping the prize so she can't use her momentum to jog away. See? She's dropping anchor," I reply, handing the wench my spyglass.

"Their cannon doors are open," she says with a gasp.

As I rip the spyglass from her gloved hands to see for myself, she yells over my shoulder. "Drop the anchor! Open the doors and ready the cannons!"

"That's my job! If we drop anchor, we'll have to raise it before we board her," I whisper through clenched teeth. I shake the spyglass at her like a paddle I'm threatening to spank her with until she pries it from my fingers. Then, to my deck, I yell, "Open the doors and ready the cannons. Don't drop the anchor!"

The message loses something when it's halfway down the deck before the words leave my lips. I scowl at the irritant stealing my thunder, but she's looking through my spyglass. My pudding-headed mateys drop the anchor chains on deck and scamper back to their position inside the gunnery's trench.

The Spanish Galleon quietly awaits her fate. Her doors are open, but her cannons aren't at the ready. She's waiting for our Jolly Roger to climb the flagpole or another Union Jack. If she fires at us and we're English, a peace treaty will dissolve. If she fires at us and we're French, they will be rewarded when they return home. If we raise the Jolly Roger or a Yellow Jack, they will open fire to defend their lives. Our captain's quarters have a closet full of flags. We have switched sides with the treaties as often as landlubbing mollies change their wigs with the fashion.

"What are you waiting for?" The wench whispers, handing me the spyglass for a glimpse before she rips it from my hands again. "Why isn't their captain on the deck?"

"What do you mean? If they're military, their captain is the sailor with more feathers than a peacock sticking from his hat. If they are merchants, the captain—"

"There is a feathered hat on deck, but it sits on a man without medals on his uniform. The man covered in finery ditched his hat in favor of the crow's nest," she says, handing me the spyglass.

Well, shiver me timbers. She's as sharp as she's tenacious and irritating. Captain hides amongst the crows while some poor sod wears his ostentatious hat on deck. That yellow-bellied criminal isn't worth the bullet, but I can't have him surprising us either.

"Greenhorn, snipe their scout," I shout. The message travels across the ratlines and up the sails to Greenhorn, who sits in our crow's nest with a long rifle.

What I wouldn't give for an experienced man to be in Greenhorn's place?! In the good ol'days, we had Sharp as our sniper. True to his name, Greenhorn's young age and lack of practice with a rifle take center stage when he misses the shot. The bullet doesn't just sail into the abyss but rips a gaping hole in their main sail that would attract the attention of anyone for miles…not excluding the turkeys on deck.

They spring into action, readying cannons, locking doors, and running to their battle stations. Their planned battle positions give away their training as military, but they don't wear uniforms or carry navy-issued weapons.

"Raise the Jolly Roger," I yell in unison with my female shadow. Bodies scramble like ants across the Galleon's deck as I gaze through the spyglass. The captain in the crow's nest spins around with his arms whirling. Perhaps he's considering flying off his doomed vessel? "Greenhorn, fire again! Her doors are open!"

As Greenhorn misses a second time, splintering the bottom of the Galleon's crow's nest, the Spanish fire her cannons. The shots drop into the drink a few yards from our hull.

A warning shot.

"Fire!" I yell, and our cannons shoot true. A line of fifteen holes mars the side of the Galleon. More people scurry from hole to hole inside the boat.

"Fire!" The second command to fire comes from the wench, and I'll be a grogblossom if my nutmegs don't follow her orders as true as mine. Even Greenhorn shoots one more time. Their Captain falls from the Crow's nest to Davey Jones's locker.

"Full sails to her. It's time to go on account!" I yell. The enemy fires, and the stair railing to the forecastle deck explodes to shower us in splinters. The wench grabs my elbow and presses against me. Her eyes are round with fear on her whitened face.

"You didn't say you would board her! I thought if you made enough holes in their boat, they would hand over the loot!"

"Which is why I'm the Captain," I sneer, shaking her off my arm. "Ready the lines to tie the prize to our decks. We're taking all she has before we sink her."

My crew cheers as my female companion cries

into her gloves. I shove her toward the kitchen as I leave the forecastle deck for the ratlines. My longsword cools my palm as I unsheathe it from my belt. A good captain always leads the charge over the rail—even Magda the she-devil flew into enemy territory first. My crew pats my shoulders and shakes my free hand as I pass. I'm fifteen feet off the ground when the irritating wench joins me. She's commandeered Chub's cat-o-nine tails as her weapon of choice…odd. Why she wouldn't grab a pistol on her way to the kitchen is beyond me.

"It's not too late to hide below with Catalina—"

"If you die before rescuing my sister, I have nothing," she says with a firm set to her mouth and fire blazing in her eyes. We drop from the rigging into the gunnery trench. My crew stares at the wench as if they've never seen a woman before. "I have nothing to lose."

"Suit yourself," I quip as my crew tosses the gangplanks between the two boats.

Ropes armed with wicked hooks sail from the gunnery trenches to the neighboring deck. Anticipation of the fight buzzes amongst me hearties, connecting us with a bolt of lightning. The smell of blood, sweat, and gunpowder fills my nose as my body remembers every passage I've had over the rail. The boat rocks and groans as she fights the tethers like a bucking horse unwilling to shed her freedom without a battle.

"Hold steady," I warn my young, inexperienced crew. I love every one of them, and if one of their empty heads pops above the railing, the enemy will blow it off. "Wait for the quiet."

Enemy sailors yell at one another in Spanish. Their boots thump on their deck.

My hair whips around my head, so I tuck the errant strands behind my ear...

Greenhorn mistakes my tick for a signal. He climbs on a line from the crow's nest and soars over our heads to the opposing boat. With his single-shot pistol in one hand and the rope in the other, he will hit their deck with one chance to kill every enemy aboard. His sword is sheathed in his belt. My jaw hits the bilge as I helplessly gape at the blooming idiot. His roar is drowned out by a chorus of gunfire.

"Charge," I yell to send our crew over the railing to help him. Bodies cross the gangplanks, jump from our rigging, and fly across the ocean as pirates fling themselves onto the Galleon.

Shots ring out over my head as Chub fires a long gun from behind the wheel, and Catalina fires her long gun from behind the kitchen door. He'll spank the daylights out of her for joining the fray. But when she sends Greenhorn's grappling opponent to the pearly gates, I thank my lucky stars she didn't listen to Chub.

Walk the Walk

Book 5: Hooking Captain Teeth

The poor youngster had no idea of his error until his boots hit the deck. His vacant stare and slow movements undermine his bravado. He will go into shock before this battle is finished.

My sword clangs as it cuts through the brass cups of the soldier's swords. Each man is disarmed and dispatched in seconds—that's why I've held onto this sword for my entire career. I stole it from a drunken ogre and built my upper body muscles until I could carry it one-handed. Under Blackbeard, my skinny frame swung the blade wildly with two hands and my eyes closed. Now, the blade doesn't leave my right hand as I stare down my next opponent…as the life drains from my current one. Speaking of my next opponent, what happened to that irritating wench? Is she cowering in the gunnery trench, crying into her skirts?

I rear back to slash the man who locked swords with me across the throat and dodge the spurt of blood from his jugular before daring to scan the decks.

A pair of officers stand back-to-back in front of the captain's quarters. Don't they know the captain fell from the crow's nest into the drink? Or do they hide another secret to this Galleon that's not military but full of soldiers? Two soldiers flank me with sissy-pitched battle cries. I behead one with my longsword before firing my one-shot pistol at the other.

Sigh. Time to reload the little bastard.

I better help Eze, who's engaged them in combat with the help of a handful of his closest mates. Once you fly the ratlines and share a sail with a group of guys, you're brothers. However, my green mateys are no match for officers who carry colonial cup hilt rapiers with steel hilts. Those don't snap under the pressure of our thicker swords and axes.

Dammit, a short soldier rushes me, and I'm forced to wrap my arm around his neck. With my sword sheathed, a cotton wad in one hand and my pistol dangling from the other, I snap his neck with my elbow.

"Boys," yells the wench as she races past me. "Yoohoo, boys!"

She skids to a stop before the officers. The sailors and pirates are a foot taller than her, but her dainty, feminine voice halts them mid-battle. Tucking her cat-o-nine tails under her elbow, she rips apart her blouse and tears down her chemise with both hands. Sweet, innocent cotton flutters to the deck like the white flag of surrender…taking the tongues from every man's mouth. With deadly accuracy, she unfurls her weapon and wraps the leather around the sailors' necks. As they watch her dairy swing with hungry eyes, she tightens her noose and cracks their necks.

Bloody hell. The two bodies fall into the arms of

my pirates, ending the battle before it starts.

"Where did you learn to fight like that?"

"My sister," she says with a shake of her head. "She likes to flash the smarts out of men's heads for sport, but she isn't a pirate if that's what you think."

"And the cat-o-nine's work? Did she teach you that as well?" If I hadn't found my lady love, the wench's mysterious sister would be right up my alley. As it stands, Sabs and Catalina would love to make friends with a woman like her.

"Oh no, that move was instinct," the wench says, accepting Eze's help to rewind her weapon. "My other form is a Kraken. This boat is yours to loot, and now you can help me save Sabrina. She's in trouble and sent me—her sister, Bettina—to you."

"Sink the boat—we're returning to Trinidad!" My crew freezes in place and looks at me with a thousand questions swimming in their eyes. Out of respect, no one voices their objections, but I owe them more than a barked order. "Got ahead of myself. Eze and your lot—check what the officers protected in the captain's quarters. Barrel, take a group and empty the armory."

"I'll lead Greenhorn and the group on the forecastle deck to clear out the kitchen," Chub says from behind me. Catalina stands in his place at our helm with the master of cannons, who I still can't name. "You don't have to ask. A quality quartermaster reads the mind of his captain."

Bloody cheek.

A strumpet from Maude's tavern spills out of the captain's quarters and onto the deck. She holds her dairy in one arm while yanking her corset down to cover her marriage box with the other. Her rouge and lip smear blot the wooden planks—probably leaving permanent circles behind.

"Please, Teeth," she begs until I bristle at her using my familiar name. "Please, Captain, have mercy. I was hired on as their doxie less than a day ago. I'll tell you everything I heard them say if you let me live. I'll service your crew. I'll kiss your toes—"

I back away as she crawls toward me. With her familiarity, I'm sure she's ridden my sugarstick in the distant past. She's a pitiful creature really, slinking along the floor like a used handkerchief. Eze approaches her on silent feet. His dagger is poised above her head as he awaits my signal. She hasn't a clue how close she is to death's door.

I peek at Sabrina's sister with a side-eye. She winds her whip around her elbow as if the fate of this woman is none of her concern. My future sister-in-law is cold as ice.

"We will take you back to Trinidad where you can return to Maude's employ—" I pause for Eze to sheathe his dagger "—but stay away from my toes and quarters. Eze will be your shadow. Give him the secrets you overheard and whatever else you planned to share with me."

I don't know who is happier, the former doxie or my ratline climber. He's taken more shifts watching the wheel while we parlay ashore than any other crew member. It's time to give him a job that's not a hardship to even the scales. As the pair scramble across the gangplank, I supervise the looting of the ship.

"Do you have a plan to rescue Sabrina?" *Please say yes.* Please let this irritating wench say she needs firepower or blades to cut down foes to size.

"Then what would I need pirates for?" The hope shining in her eyes is sharper than her cutthroat fighting style.

"Chub," I call as he approaches the gangplank with a flour sack on each shoulder. The top of the burlap is chin height despite its lofted perch on my friend. What he lacks in height, he more than makes up in brains and brawn—which is what I need. "We're meeting with Bettina in the captain's quarters once we cut this boat loose. We need a plan. Sabrina's in trouble."

"Aye, aye, Captain!"

Chapter 11

Sabrina

I die tonight, and I'm oddly comforted by the fact. This show is the last time Barnabie will pull my hair, grab my tentacles, and fondle my breasts while the audience laughs and cheers. The weights on my wrists make it impossible for me to fight him. My humiliation ends tonight when the full moon rises. The tentacles that landed me in this freak show will fuse into two legs. The leering men in the crowd—including Pastor Richard, who attended alone—will finally take a glimpse of my cunt as my drowned human form floats to the surface of my tank. I hope they enjoy the view.

Despite my early demise, I have no regrets. I loved hard and whored harder. I used my human and Kraken form to bring joy to myself in everything I did. Teeth, my soulmate, sails in search of me…but he'll figure out I'm gone. *Eventually.* The thought of my hot-blooded pudding-head makes me smile. He's free.

Walk the Walk

Book 5: Hooking Captain Teeth

On the high seas, he's above the law and conquered time by becoming a legend. Everyone knows and fears Captain Teeth. As Barnabie holds me aloft from my tank, shaking me so my dairy jiggles, I grin like a grogblossom because Barnabie is a quarter of the man he wants to portray. His stories puff himself, but never to the stature of Captain Teeth.

"When I lifted the beast from the depths of hell, imagine my surprise. The mighty Kraken was but a little girl—no match for me, eh lads?" Barnabie's question is answered by a chorus of laughter. The humiliation used to bother me, but soon, I will be free.

I lock eyes with Pastor Richard. Without a brood of orphans or my gorgeous sister to distract him, his attention is locked on me. He sipped from a flask during the others' presentations, but not mine. Leaning forward, eyes wide and hands folded over his tented trousers, I'm his singular focus. I'm as confused as I am disgusted. My sister walks on legs, so he must have consumed her soulbeak. She wouldn't have given it to anyone else, nor would she have accidentally lost it in a casual ride on the St. George. If he accepted her soul and chose for them to live as humans, then why isn't he making children with her in his drafty chapel? Why does he hunger for me when he has my sister in his bed?

Or does he? I long for one more conversation

with Bettina to be certain she will be okay when I'm gone.

Barnabie releases the leash and my hair, so I slither into my tank. I open my gills to suck the clean water through them. My traveling tank stinks with rot, and I've transferred some to this tank. The sudden churning of the water kicks up my waste from the bottom. I have a few precious breaths before the contamination spreads the rancid taste.

Dolbie and Rufus wheel my enclosure to the farthest wall so the patrons can wander around the four exhibits. Tonight, I'm on display—like every night—with the bearded lady, a man with a lion face, a four-armed woman, and a man who stands less than a foot tall. Where does Barnabie find these people? Were they stolen like me?

I count five men who walk with obvious military posture in plain clothes. The remarks and gestures the men made at my tank used to scare me until one took it too far in Nassau, and the hidden security sprang into action. They protect Barnabie's treasures. Will one of them release me from the tank when my gills vanish and I drown? Will they be able to lift me when the eight weights on my tentacles reduce to two weights on my ankles?

The sky blushes from the blue of twilight to a rosy hue. I gaze at my last sunset through the door flap to the tent until some impossibly tall man blocks my view. He wears a giant feathered hat, which adds to his impressive height. The harlot on his arm enters first. No honest woman would wear feathers on her piled-high hair or a shocking red dress cinched at mid-thigh…except maybe me. She brings a smile to my face as I'm overcome with nostalgia. Her hair is red like mine, so I can put my younger self in her shoes.

Pastor Richard stops his advance to my tank to gawk at the beauty.

She's striking. She's stunning.

She's my prissy, stick-up-her-arse sister!

Her tall companion ducks through the tent flap and out of the sun's masking glare. He tips his hat at the bearded lady, who blushes at his attention. Blond hair glides over his wide shoulders. The hand he holds over his sheathed sword has four fingers. I bet the hand in his jacket, as if it holds braces—not a gun's butt, has three fingers. A plain townswoman fans herself as he bows to step around her and her portly husband. I carefully school my face to avoid giving away the ruse. Oh, my soul, Captain Teeth's muscular body, cleaned and dressed to the nines, is exactly what I hoped would be the last vision I see.

That answers my questions about Bettina's relationship with Pastor Richard and how she will survive without me. She will take my place at Teeth's side. They look like they belong together if you ignore how she holds her belly, fisting her flimsy dress. Her rejected soulbond to Richard must hurt like hell. If I get one message to Teeth, it will be to keep Bettina as far away from Trinidad as possible. With distance, the soulbond fades, but it roars to life when they share the same room.

I open my mouth in hopes Teeth can lip-read when he runs a finger down the glass over my face. He repeats the action on the left seam of the tank. He flicks his eyes to the finger. Oh! I'm supposed to follow his movements like we're playing a game. I sway my upper body to the left edge, careful not to touch the film on the wall. He repeats the finger smear in the center and then the right seam. My body follows like a charmed snake in a basket. In reality, my behavior isn't too far from the truth. I've tuned out the room as my soul focuses on his expression of deep concentration.

"She looks to be your twin," Rufus sneers at Bettina.

"You ain't be hiding tentacles under your skirts," Dolbie sneers, licking his cracked lips.

"Where would I hide them? This dress is a little flutter of nothing," Bettina says, lifting it to flash her garters at them.

"Open the tank," Teeth says in an icy whisper that sends a shiver down my tentacles. "Release the

Kraken, and I will take her quietly."

"Not on your life!" Rufus shouts while Dolbie searches for Barnabie. The nutmegs can't make such a decision without the boss's say-so, even though Teeth holds a flintlock pistol at waist height.

"Oh, it will be your life," Teeth whispers. This time, both my abusers anxiously scan the crowd for Barnabie.

"Bettina," Richard scolds, interrupting Teeth's rescue. "What are you wearing? Don't you realize Christ is always watching? People will think you have forsaken our Savior!"

"Richard, I haven't forsaken anything," Bettina sneers in a voice I've never heard her use. "But have you? Were you performing for your savior when you rubbed your sugarstick as my sister was tortured on stage, or was it for the amusement of your new wife? I didn't see her when I entered, but if she's in attendance, I must say hello. She will want to hear my tricks to get you off faster."

"You're a monster—"

"Maybe that's why you climaxed in my mouth so quickly…even though you never saw my monster form. Perhaps your pious little wife is a lost cause—"

Richard turns beet red and lunges at Bettina. She gasps with her hand over her bosom like the weak little flower she is. I blink frantically at Teeth to save her, but he's absorbed in finding the tank's weaknesses. Why does he think Bettina can hold her own? How do I tell him she's not fierce like me without giving away to the handlers that I know them?

Teeth steps out of Richard's way. He tucks his gun into his holster with a sleight of hand. I wouldn't have noticed the maneuver had I not been studying him already. What's caused him to hide the pistol?

"We'll have none of that," rumbles one of the disguised officers. He grabs Richard by the collar and drags him to the tent's exit flap. They must wait for a short, red-haired man and his buxom companion to enter.

"Five!" Teeth's shout startles my heart from my chest. Five what? Five holes in the tank, five seams to cut, or five minutes until I transform?

"Aye, aye," yells the couple at the entrance as the man pulls a machete from his belt.

Richard lunges for the well-endowed lady, who stabs her tiny knife into his throat. She shrieks, which alerts her companion. With a slash of his machete, Richard's guts spill onto the ground. He trembles as he drops and flops about like a fish out of water.

The lady steps over Richard's flailing body as she retrieves her knife. Blood splashes on her lacy dress and shiny boots. I can't believe my eyes when threads burst from her wrists to wrap around two other plainclothes officer's necks. As they struggle with the bonds, their heads turn purple. The lady leans back to tighten them as her short companion fights his way through the excited crowd with his machete raised. As he beheads the first disguised security man, the lady sags with exhaustion against the tent.

Clouds form in my peripheral vision. I force my gills to open, but they are shrinking into my rounded hips. The cuffs of six weights plunk to the sand as my tentacles absorb into my legs. I claw at the glass to lift myself to the top. My neck strains as I tip my head back as far as possible. When my lips breach the surface, I heave and cough. My arms paddle with the weights resting in my palms.

I don't know how long I will last.

"Aye, aye," is shouted from all around as the tent is pierced in a ring at the top. Sword points extend a foot through the canvas as they rip down the sides. The tent flaps in ribbons as the loose pieces fall to the ground. A pirate steps through each of the new openings, surrounding the show's occupants. They pull women and children from the tent's confines so the presumed innocent can scamper home without injury.

"Aye, aye," yells Bettina, to my astonishment. She removes a cat-o-nine tails from her waistline. I thought it was a decorative belt, but as she whirls the leather around her head, I know better. She copies my favorite way to drag sailors from their boats but uses the whip instead of a tentacle. The leather wraps around a disguised officer's neck as he rushes toward Teeth. She tugs it to the left to sweep the man off his feet. Instead of hitting the gentle waves of the Caribbean like the sailors I torment, he crashes to the unforgiving dirt floor. Blood puddles bloom around his still form.

As the strength drains from my aching arms, I smile with pride at her.

"Chub, Catalina, free the prisoners on your side," Teeth calls over the mele. A tingle resonates through my bones with the volume, authority, and overall timbre of his voice.

"Aye, aye," replies the spider lady and her companion.

"Eze," Teeth calls to the tallest man on the north side of the tent. "Free the gentleman closest to you."

"Aye, Captain," he yells as he sheathes his short sword. Another pirate steps close to his left side to cover him. The two men hold fingers in their ears as Eze shoots off the lock.

The shot is louder than expected as Teeth shoots the lock off my tank. His furrowed brow presses against the glass as he checks on me. My lungs seize as water flows down my throat. Not enough air. My thoughts cloud. When did my limbs become so heavy?

I blow a kiss to see him smile one last time before my eyes drift closed.

Chapter 12

Captain Teeth

"Lift off the lid, or my next shot will blow your nutmegs into pudding," I whisper to the idiots guarding Sabrina's tank.

Between her sister's drama and the late arrival of me hearties up the tent's rigging, this has taken far too long. The whistles of the local authorities sing along the streets. That's what I get for allowing the children to go free—and the mothers to whose skirts they clung. One of those buggers went to the lobster soldiers and local devils on patrol. If we don't wish to find ourselves in hempen necklaces while hanging from the Sheriff's picture frame, we must get aboard and weigh anchor.

"Not so fast," says a slimy little man over my shoulder. The confidence in his eyes flares when his security stooge holds a knife to my Adam's apple. "This is my show, and these animals are my property."

"Animals?" Bettina's sputter of rage comes out

faster than my mind can go. "This human woman is an animal?"

I step aside so the larger man can see Sabs lying in her tank. She's an excellent actress. I almost believe she's conked out. Blimey, she lives in the ocean. Certainly, she breathes underwater? Perhaps she looks dead because she breathes like a shark and her mouth is closed…sharks hold their mouths open.

"My Kraken!" The little man's shouts rush my blood, pulsing at my temples.

She's *mine*.

I unsheathe my dagger and press it to his bulbous belly. "My lady love needs air. Now call off your man and open her tank, or I'll gut you like a fish."

"You wouldn't! My security will have your head," he shouts, raining spittle down the bottom half of my shirt.

"Catalina," I yell. Silky threads wrap around the security guard's neck and wrist.

"What's this?" He yells as his dagger falls through his fingers. His opposite hand claws the tether. From across the room, Catalina weaves a lattice between his neck and wrist. If he yanks his wrist hard enough, he may strangle himself. Avast ye! I love what Chub and Catalina have devised to protect her in a fight.

"This is your exit or your last stand," I say with

my namesake smile. "Your choice."

Yellow-bellied, giant landlubber steps backward.

"You can't leave me," the shorter man blubbers. "We have a contract."

"Not enforceable by colonial law. I know the generals," the guard says as he turns on his heel. He stomps to the perimeter with his wrist hanging from his neck. He grabs himself in a hand necklace to save face, but me hearties laugh as he passes. I nod to the ratline climber holding the perimeter to allow him to disappear into the night.

"Tank's open," stammers one of the tank's attendants.

Sabrina doesn't stir with the jostling of the water. My heart races. I knock on the glass. Her hair waves around her hips, but otherwise, she's still as a marble statue. Panic, bile, and my last sip of rum surge up my throat.

"No!" I yell, kicking my leg over the side of the tank.

The wooden frame creaks and groans as I hoist my body over the lip. My right boot absorbs the putrid water. Bracing each knee against the ledge, I rip off my holster and leather duster. Hat be damned, but a water-logged pistol is useless to anyone. Before my items hit the floor, my upper half dives into the murky water. I gather my lady love in my arms.

So light and delicate in her human form…did her ribs always stick out like this? They didn't the last time I held her Kraken body. I memorized every inch of her. Pressing her chest to chest, I feel every knob and ridge of her skeleton. I doubt she's eaten much in the last few weeks while I scoured the seas for her. My hand cradles her head to my shoulder, wishing her breath teased my neck.

I topple over the side, landing on my dry left boot. Bettina shoves the show's master backward so I have space to lay Sabs flat on her back. I press her belly up and under her ribs in an old waterlogging remedy. Half me hearties owe their life to this maneuver, for all greenhorns seem to struggle with staying *on* the boat. If only it would save Sabs. She gurgles with each thrust, so I turn her head to the side. Her sister removes a pin from her hair to pick the locks on the weights holding her wrists and ankles.

"Come on, love," I whisper as water dribbles from the corner of her mouth. "Come back to sass me. Nobody will keep me in line if my last memory of you turns me into a monster."

"She's dead," shouts the show's owner. "You owe me her worth…and the tent…and what I paid those worthless patrolmen. I'll see you hanged for this!"

"No, you won't," I say, whipping my pistol from where it lies in its holster on the ground beside me. The hole in his forehead smokes as his eyes roll toward it. I raise my elbow to catch him before he can fall onto Sabs. Bettina removes the last weight but can't seem to remove the collar. There's a locking mechanism in the ring instead of a lock hanging off of it. We need the specific tool they used to fasten the collar around Sabs's neck...or Chub's machete.

"There's no time," I whisper to her. My crew must weigh anchor before the mele in the streets breaches our perimeter. "Back to the ship! Back to the ship!"

I throw Sabs over my shoulder—hopefully, the position will continue to drain her as we run to safety. Chub and Catalina lead us with sword points forward. We're flanked by former captives and my pirates as we scuttle toward the docks. My focus is straight ahead. *Patricia's Wish* sits at the end of the dock. Her sails unfurl as her anchor rises from the deep. Greenhorn stands by the railing's edge with the gangplank resting on his shoulder.

With one arm wrapped around my lady's naked arse and my other brandishing my sword, I engage with soldiers wearing more finery than I thought existed. Where did these rich mollies come from? If it isn't their brass-handled swords that fail, it's the hands I

Walk the Walk

Book 5: Hooking Captain Teeth

slice off with my heavy, iron sword. Best item I've ever stolen! We drip water from the show's former tent to the harbor. The moans of my lady love as she recovers harden my sugarstick and hobble my gait to our boat.

Blimey, now is not the time! Why is it that every time I hold this wench, I feel the need to ink my quill in her? I thought she was dead a few minutes ago. There's something to this soulbond she's not telling me. I'm a bastard who knows every brothel's madam in the Caribbean on a first-name basis, but fighting my way off an island with my cock half-mast is a new development.

There's something about my magnificent lady love.

"Let them all aboard unless they're firing at you," I shout at Greenhorn as I leap onto the boat. The momentum slams Sabrina's belly onto my shoulder. She shites through her teeth down my back. Avast ye, not even her flashing the hash on me cools my passion.

"Aye, aye," he replies as he drops the gangplank. He grunts when Chub throws Catalina into his arms. The pair stumble backward but maintain their footing.

"Chub, get us on open water," I yell over my clean shoulder.

"Aye, aye, Captain," he yells as he runs by me to the helm.

"You're alive if you can paint my back with your innards," I say as we cross the deck to the captain's quarters. I kick the double doors open and help them close behind us. They muffle the chaos on deck to a dull roar.

"Sorry" is music to my ears. I flip her onto her back hard enough she bounces off the sheets. I take her jaw in my hands and claim her mouth as my own. My open-mouthed kisses migrate down her body as my greedy hands check for injuries. She's thin, with knots in her arm muscles where they must have yanked her around. Her skin chafes under the metal collar she still wears.

"Stop, I taste gross," she whines in a breathless tone that sets me ablaze.

"All right, Sabs—" I pause and sit up because the beaming smile she gives me when I call her by her nickname takes my breath away "—you win this time. If death can't keep my cock deflated, we will have a hell of a time getting acquainted."

"Acquainted?"

"Yes," I say, running my sparse fingers through her hair because I can't help touching her. "You say we're soulmates. Our attraction is incredible, but I'd like to be friends too. I want to dance with you on deck, introduce you to me hearties, and watch the sunrise."

"I never took you for a romantic," she replies,

squirming under my gaze. I lift the bed's black coverlet, a remnant of the vampiress who decorated the room, over Sabrina's shivering body. Her sigh of contentment as she snuggles warms my heart.

"I am romantic, fun, hilarious—"

"Humble?" The twist of her lips and the flash of sass in her eyes threaten to turn the contents of my britches to stone.

"Never humble," I say with a chuckle. "A humble captain will acquire a blackspot in his first days on the job. You are only as powerful as the stories say you are. That power is what keeps your crew believing they will live through the trials of the sweet trade—hurricanes, boat damage, sickness, engaging with prizes, and the trials of everyday life on the ship. I swear, someone flies off the rigging and into the drink every damn day."

"They do," she replies with a giggle. "I've pushed many of their arses to the surface in the years I followed your boat."

"Why didn't you say something to get my attention? All those years lost—"

"I hated you." Ouch, there's a dagger to me heart.

"Oh," is all I can say.

"You humiliated me, Teeth. We shared promises of love and commitment that night. The next morning, you couldn't get away from me fast enough. You treated me like I was less than human, *without* knowing I was a Kraken shifter. How could I open up to you and give you a chance to accept my dual nature if you couldn't accept me as a fellow human being?"

"Oh Sabs," I whisper as the tightening in my chest pushes the breath from my lungs. "I was young and stupid. While I don't remember our exact interaction, I can tell you it was a transaction that got out of hand. I wasn't mature enough for emotional bonds—not ready for something real. You had every right to hate me, but now I'm begging for a chance to make things right between us."

"Begging?"

I slide off the bed so one knee hits the wooden floor. Her slender hand is cold as I wrap mine around it. My palms rub her hand vigorously to bring forth her blood. We stare at one another in comfortable silence, our feelings passing through the warm gaze in our eyes.

"I'm not a learned man. I've never taken life seriously and rose to this position through the support of men smarter than me. My mistakes outweigh my triumphs, and my story is a complete farse. The formidable Captain Teeth is Milton Gladstone, and he lays down his sword at your feet."

"Milton? Milton?" Her giggles break the boulder

lodged in my chest. "No wonder you never fought your pirate nickname."

"First of all, Milton is a wonderful name…for someone else. Secondly, Blackbeard named me Teeth, and nobody argues with Blackbeard."

"Your missing fingers demonstrate your experience when arguing with Blackbeard. They show you are mighty brave."

"Thank you, my lovely, but they also demonstrate how stupid I was in my youth. But I digress. Thirdly, my nickname has saved my arse more times than I can count. Pirates of rival ships long to knock a tooth from Teeth's mouth, so they aim for my face. I learned to slice their yellow underbellies when I entered the fray, ducking such egotistical foolery."

"Whatever works. I could listen to your stories all day."

"I can't promise a secure, quiet life of farming in some small hamlet or a safe, bustling life as a merchant's wife, but I promise to keep you entertained for the rest of our days. Be more than the monster who holds my tethers—be my wife, Sabrina."

"I wouldn't last a day on a farm or in a tiny shop in a forgotten village. No matter what life you choose for us, I will need my time in the sea," she says, twisting the bed covers around her opposite hand's fingers. Why is she nervous? I laid my heart at her feet.

What isn't she telling me?

"You are never leaving my sight again," I growl between kisses to her knuckles.

"We both know I can't keep that promise," she whispers, running her fingers through my dripping hair to soften her words.

"We will find a way, or my name's not Captain Teeth!" I glare into her sea-green eyes until they fill with tears. Her bittersweet smile breaks my heart. After tonight, she will be a Kraken again and need seawater more than my embrace.

"There's a way," Bettina says from the doorway.

"Sis, please don't—"

"Captain, your crew needs you," she says, leaning against the threshold. "There was something in the captain's log of the last prize that Chub wants you to see, and the rest, well…they need direction."

I'm conflicted until I read the anxiety on Sabrina's face. Perhaps her sister can talk some sense into her. What could keep us apart when she calls me her soulmate? She throws this soulbond in my face when admonishing me for my past deeds but forsakes it when I talk of the future. If I were a cleverer man, I could decipher the puzzle. Too bad I'm too embarrassed of my actions to confide in Chub.

"Bettina, will you keep her resting while I get things sorted?" I ask the question as I rise to my feet.

My knees scream in protest as I hide my pain behind a pirate's mask of bravado. I drop my water-logged hat, duster, and shirt over the desk tucked into the corner of my room.

"Aye, aye," she replies with a note of sarcasm.

"Then I will check in with Chub, set our course, and return with food—" My clean, dry shirt is another layer of armor. No one can see my vulnerability but Sabrina. It would send me walking the plank—hearties or not. We don't disrespect women on this boat, and the female members of my crew would put me to trial for the way my younger self treated Sabrina. I'm guilty as sin, so I would lose in a heartbeat.

"Oh, please, don't force me to eat. The most delicious food would taste horrible—"

"Madam, you are on a pirate ship. I guarantee the food will taste horrible, but dry hardtack will settle the storm in your belly," I say at the door.

"You're better off feeding her raw fish," Bettina replies, crossing the room to sit on the bed. "A Kraken lives on a diet of raw fish."

"I'm on the hunt," I say with a bow. I will leave them to their secrets as long as they put me in the best light possible. From the cartographer's room below, Chub and I will hear every word. Now that I have Sabrina on my boat, I'll be hard-pressed to let her go.

Chapter

13

Sabrina

"You want to talk about him?" She asks casually. As if I'm answering any of her questions.

"You've been on legs for days," I say with more hurt than sharpness laced in my voice. I wish I could scold her the way she lectures me. She messed up in the worst way possible. I'm angry with her for throwing away her chance at true love while accusing me of doing the same thing. "My soulbeak rests on my navel. Does yours?"

"No," she says to her lap.

"What to tell me about it?"

"No."

"No lecture to prevent me from making the same mistake? I'm as surprised by that as I am by your get-up," I add to lighten the mood. As angry as I am at her, she's hurting more than me. The rings of sadness haunted her eyes as she entered the show's tent on Teeth's arm—not when Richard lost his head.

"Oh, this old thing? We found a trunk of women's clothes on the ship we plundered before your rescue. I thought it would give Richard impure thoughts when he's with his wife. Revenge is a sin, but my definitions of sin and purity are upside-down."

"Wife? What happened? I thought he was the one for you." I dab her eyes with the corner of the bed's coverlet.

"I gave him everything…" Her sniffles escalate into sobs.

I peel back the stack of quilts and blankets to invite her to join me. We wrap our arms around one another as she cries in my hair. I let her wails fill the room as she shatters. My soulbeak tingles with sympathy. The heavy, black curtains on the portholes wave as mourning flags signal over a fort. Even the boat slows its momentum to listen to Bettina's troubles. If Richard weren't dead already, the crew would rally around her.

Then why am I terrified of them? Bettina huddles under the quilts to hide from her troubles, but I wish to hide from the humans. I trust Bettina and Teeth because my soulbeak links my soul to theirs. If they plotted to return me to a show, my belly would sour. Since Chub seemed to be the brains behind my rescue and Catalina killed Richard on Bettina's behalf, I guess I can trust them as well. However, there are lots of humans on this boat…in tight quarters…

Will the nightmares of my time in captivity ever allow me to frolic on deck? Have I lost the sparkle that makes me Sabrina? Will it return when I shift into a Kraken and swim away? How can I see Teeth again if I can't be on his boat? My anxiety begs me to focus on Bettina's problems instead of breaking my heart with my own. Whether I swim away as a Kraken or live my days in this room, Bettina must be settled in a life she enjoys…without me.

"What did you give Richard exactly?" I ask when she runs out of tears and silence replaces her cries.

"Last month, we put the kids to bed and spread a blanket behind the chapel to stargaze. He told me biblical stories, which became personal stories as the night grew late. I was so overcome with the openness of his heart that I made love to him, but it wasn't love on his end. The next morning, I broke my soulbeak into his breakfast—hurt like hell, but I didn't want to wait—and floated the idea of shifters in the congregation by him. He raged in a powerful tableside sermon about the abomination of shifters. He called us demons, Sabrina."

"With such a tirade, the soulbond decided you would spend your life on legs. Did you take his plate away and smash it over his head?"

"I should have, but I was stunned. What happened to the inclusion of all God's creatures and mercy for those less fortunate—"

"Did you see us as less fortunate as Krakens? Are you happier now as a human?" I suppress the hurt in my voice, but I'm proud to be a Kraken. I like who I am and thought Bettina was secure in herself too. If I return to my Kraken form forever, will she respect my choice?

"Not anymore," she says bitterly. Her fierceness shouldn't set my heart at ease, but it does. "His hunger for your Kraken broke something in me. He wanted you. Despite his preaching, he desired a Kraken's touch. On the outside, he acted as the beacon of purity, but his rotten insides held many dirty secrets—including his affair with me. I didn't know his mission was funded by his wealthy wife, who has spent the last few years on a different island. While she devoted herself to helping the poor, Richard devoted himself to me…and a few other women in the village…and his visits to Maude's tavern."

"Oh Betts, I'm so sorry," I whisper, hugging her closer. I stroke her hair while my brain spins with possible things to say. Do I tell her she's better off without him? She's a destitute human. He doomed her to life as one of the helpless people he supposedly lifted from poverty. Do I tell her I can't choose for us to be humans together? I can't because of what I endured at the hands of Barnabie, Rufus, Dolbie, and the random men they allowed to touch me during the shows.

What does this mean for Teeth and me? How can I ask her what to say to his proposal when she's ruined and needs my support?

Knock, knock.

"Come in," I shout, hoping it's not Teeth. He can't enter this chamber of sorrow with his flowery promises of love. It would rub Bettina's nose in the filth of Richard's sins.

"I must say you will be the easiest person to serve on the boat," Catalina chirps as she enters the room. She carries a large tray that contains two heaping plates of flopping fish and three tankards. "The guys caught the fish and dropped them onto the plate. I didn't have to lift a finger beyond pouring the grog. Seems too late in the day for tea—especially after the thrilling evening we've had. If you don't mind the company, I thought I'd join you for a drink and answer your questions on the sweet trade."

"The least we can do is share a drink. I owe you one," Bettina says, climbing from the bed to the wardrobe. She grabs a long, threadbare coat and tosses it at me. Hmmm, it smells of Teeth…err, Milton…I just can't call him that horrid name…Teeth's scent.

The worn leather is buttery soft against my skin.

"Owe me one? How do you know?" Catalina splutters as she sets Teeth's table with our meal. I breathe a sigh of relief when the door closes behind her without adding more visitors. Beyond an eyebrow quirk, she doesn't ask me about the reaction.

"I saw you stab Pastor Richard. If you hadn't done it, I'd find a way to stab him," Bettina says, wrapping her arm around Catalina in a brief hug.

"Oh, that," Catalina whispers, blushing fiercely. "I thought you meant mending the shirt you tore in the battle. The buttons weren't recovered from the ship we sank, but the new lace panels should cover your dairy. I brought it as a peace offering in case you were mad my Chub killed your friend."

"That cheating, rotten, self-righteous son of a biscuit-eater is no friend of mine. And any woman brave enough to stab him while her man beheads him is the type of woman I want in my circle of friends."

"Hey, I recognize that lace," I say, scrambling out of bed to the table. I wrap Teeth's duster around me, but the hem drags on the floor, and the shoulders hang off my elbows. At the table, I finger the fresh panels on Battina's blouse. "That pattern has Pintarro rosettes. Half the women in the Caribbean would give their fingers to weave lace in those rosettes—makes the shirt skyrocket in value."

"Because I'm Catalina Pintarro, or at least I will be until I marry Chub." She releases the blouse to my care and points her wrist at me. My eyes bug out like a grouper's when five thin lines burst from the spinnerets under her skin. A swirling pattern of waves weaves Teeth's buttonholes to the rusty buttons, closing the duster around me. The masculine garment is transformed with feminine finery so delicate, it resembles the foam that caresses the beach.

If Teeth is attached to this duster one iota…he will hate it.

I beam at my spidery new best friend. A deluge of warmth, calm, and security surround me. I'm as safe in this coat as I am in Teeth's arms.

"If you are the owner of Pintarro Textiles, you must shite money. Why are you a pirate?" I don't know what's funnier, Bettina's question or listening to a curse cross her prissy lips. She pulls out a chair and joins Catalina at the table, leaving two chairs empty.

"Because your dinner companions have found the secret to living happily ever after. Their futures are best compared to fairy tales," says Teeth from the doorway. He leans on the frame with a fire in his eyes as he scans the duster adorning my body. While the lace closes the coat, its open weave allows him a forbidden glimpse at my dairy and cunt as I move.

"Oh really, Captain, please enlighten me. Since

I failed at love, tell me, what's the secret to charming a prince into my bed like in the fairytales?" Bettina shoves a small fish into her mouth and chews as the tail flaps along her lips. Silly sister thinks she can disgust Teeth. I've kept the sordid details on his manners from her…or she wouldn't make such a mistake.

"Why bed a charming prince when you can have a dirty pirate?" He reaches down his leathers to adjust his erection. Catalina and Bettina laugh, but I can't help the familiar hunger growing between my legs. I sit to squeeze my thighs together. As much as I wish to learn about my soulmate's personality, I'd rather study his relentless arousal in my presence. "Seriously, Betts, if you are sick of the constricting island towns, you'd make an excellent pirate."

"Oh Sabrina, you should have seen your sister," Catalina chimes in. She flinches when I slurp the tentacles of a baby squid between my lips. "I watched her fearlessly jump into the battle on an enemy's deck. One flash of her dairy, and they were stunned into submission—"

"You? You flashed your dairy at enemies?" I sputter the questions at my sister. She stops yanking the spine from a second fish on her plate to nod at me. "Is that how you lost your buttons?"

"I learned from you," she says quietly. "I misjudged you, badly. I'm sorry, Sabrina."

"You were fooled by a rat who got his comeuppance…thanks to Catalina."

"A toast to Lady Catalina!" Teeth shouts into the hallway.

Cheers blast through the entry as the crew shows their love for her. She blushes a delicate pink, at odds with the bloodthirsty lady who strangles men with her spider webs.

"What's next on the agenda, Captain? Can I get married tonight?"

"First light in the morning, my love," Chub says, pushing past Teeth to enter the room. Catalina bounces from her seat to embrace the short, red-bearded man. He swings her off her feet as he buries his face in her cleavage. Her squeal of delight warms my heart…and paints a green expression of envy across Bettina's features.

How did this room become so full? Surrounded by my new family, my heart pounds in my throat. This is the happily ever after I've dreamed of since Teeth jilted me years ago. Why can't I be normal and enjoy the camaraderie? I want to throw myself overboard.

"The happy couples must make some decisions before we set sail the following day," Teeth says, entering the room with a lazy swagger. He twirls the remaining chair on one leg before straddling it. His fingers poise over my plate to steal a morsel… then retracts his hand when he finds my lunch moves on its own.

"Couples?" Bettina asks, shooting me a look of confusion.

"Chub and Catalina must decide if we will take the job promised to our last prize before we drop them off in Mexico or if it's full sails west."

"Captain, Catalina and I are at your service. We will stay aboard while you fill our crew's coffers with honest work. Maybe it'll be a spark of inspiration," Chub says with a twinkle in his eyes. He sits in Catalina's chair and pulls her onto his lap.

"What's the honest work?" I ask, ripping a shiny, spotlight parrotfish into bite-sized pieces. All eyes are poised on the fish as I casually dissect it. Several of my companions gulp their verbal hash, but unfortunately, not Teeth.

"A wealthy family in Boston wishes to dispose of a troublesome family member. Seems the eldest son is a satyr, with a satyr's appetite for quiffing high society's virgins. His human-presenting parents claim they want him to disappear not because he looks *other* but because his reputation tarnishes theirs."

"Do you believe them?" Bettina asks.

"Not in the slightest," Chub replies with a rumbling laugh. "This is a rescue staged to look like an execution. While you ladies were recovering in here, the crew voted to give the satyr a chance to learn the sweet trade and earn a spot on the boat."

"You are very kind to accept those who are *other* so readily," Bettina says softly to her half-eaten plate. Oh, I can hear the waves churning in my sister's head. On land, she'd be destitute and alone. However, on *Patricia's Wish*, she'd be one of Teeth's hearties and able to earn a living wage. She'd explore the world from within a group of supportive friends.

But where do I fit in?

"Sabrina must decide if she will accept my marriage proposal, too," Teeth declares, grabbing my hand where it rests on the table. He kisses my knuckles as my sister gapes.

"You must marry him!"

"She hasn't answered," Teeth answers in a frosty tone.

"Only because you don't know what marrying me entails," I say, dangling a slimy sand diver in front of his nose. I maintain eye contact as I suck the fish between my lips and crunch the bones as I chew. To Teeth's credit, he doesn't flinch.

"Please excuse my sister's vile table manners," Bettina scolds me with a swat under the table. "She's not used to eating at a table…because she's usually dancing on them. Her foul behavior is to scare you off—"

"Dancing on tables? Foul manners? These two deserve each other," Chub quips.

"Yes, we do," Teeth replies with his gaze focused on me. I shrink into his giant coat as he leans forward. He plucks a wiggling fish off my plate and dangles it between our noses. The words are stolen from my mouth as he drops the fish between his lips. His Adam's apple bobs as he swallows it whole. Without breaking eye contact, he swipes my tankard and drains it. "I won't let anything tear us apart."

"Really? So, what will it be—Kraken or human?" I ask as I feed him a second fish.

Chapter 14

Captain Teeth

"Lass looks a little green around the gills," Chub mutters against the lapel of his best jacket. I frown at the groom as he nods to my left.

"Catty hasn't come out of the kitchen yet," I snap.

My eyes scan the deck for something amiss. Spider webs hang from the lower booms to create sheer curtains around the ceremony. I've half a mind to store them in the captain's quarters. What if Sabrina wishes our wedding to be as sweet? The uncouth pirates in my crew hang from the ratlines with the lanterns. If not for the captain's title, I'd be lofted with them. Delicate flowers made of Catty's lace adorn the barrels and boxes that usually litter the main deck. With Eze at the helm at our backs, the ship's steady. If it isn't Catty or the boat that worries Chub…

Sabrina huddles with her sister in the direction Chub nodded. Does her dress or expression cause him concern? If she wants to wear the duster I wore as a ratline climber, she's allowed. My future wife has access to everything I own…and she looks so stinking adorable in the giant thing. Catty hadn't minded that she declined another dress, so why should Chub? Or maybe it's the way Sabrina's eyes dart around with suspicion. She's been slow to warm up to the crew, but that's to be expected after what she endured at the show. If I could gut that landlubber's corpse, I would. Whatever they did to her, their deeds stole some of the fire from her eyes.

"Give her time," I say with an exhausted sigh.

"I have time. You have time. The boat has time. But how much time until she sprouts tentacles?"

"A few hours at most," I whisper. Sabrina catches me staring and gives me a weak smile. Is she shaking all over? Her hands burrow in the draping of her sleeves, so I can't tell. "I had hoped we'd be dancing and showing Sabs how wonderful the sweet trade can be. I want her to see me hearties as our extended family—people who will protect her at all costs."

"Is that how you feel? That the sweet trade is 'wonderful?' Or is piracy just a better option than life on land?" Chub whispers.

"If she's happy, I'll have a reason to be happy as captain. Maybe I'll step into your position when we reach Mexico, or better yet—rejoin me hearties in the rigging. Perhaps it's the faking of competence that drowns me in ennui," I whisper so I don't accidentally earn myself a black spot…or a walk down the plank.

"Remember what we overheard in your cabin as the ladies readied themselves. Being Sabrina's mate gives you more choices than captain or crew member."

"I'll never apologize for eavesdropping like a henpecked dairy chaser."

"I never said you should," Chub replies with that mischievous twinkle that warns me I won't like his next words. "I'm opening your mind to a new life—"

"I refuse to settle on land—even in Mexico as your neighbor."

The band's tune changes from the sound of choking cats to something resembling a wedding march. Greenhorn, Frons, and Hash play African drums like true musicians. However, the pipes played by the bearded lady and Barrel could shatter a window.

Catty emerges from the kitchen in a dress that sparkles in the low morning sun. We'll regret the red skies this morning, but for the wedding, they are the perfect backdrop. Chub and Catty's fiery romance bloomed on the boat and will stand the test of time. I'm so happy for my best friend I could burst. It is an honor to officiate their wedding as Captain.

My eyes meet Sabrina's worried gaze. Powder,

the master of cannons, has brought his lads to the deck for the ceremony. They crowd around Bettina and Sabrina in a ring of protection…but Sabrina doesn't see them as such. The *others* from the show huddle together on the forecastle desk, as far away from the gathering as possible. Would Sabrina be more relaxed with them? Bettina has yet to notice the distress written across her sister's face. I'm torn between the decorum befitting Chub's wedding and easing the anxiety I feel radiating off my lady.

"I get a maid of honor, yeah?" Catty's question pulls me from my tormented thoughts. When did she cross the deck? I must have blanked out longer than I thought.

"You get whatever your heart desires—" Chub's dairy-chasing promises are cut off by the lacy bouquet Catty shoves under his chin. Pointy fabric flowers embed themselves in his beard and tug his head when he tries to lower the bastards. His grunt summons laughter from the audience until he silences it with a glare. He may be the groom, but he's also the boss…after me.

"Stand with me," Catty says, tugging Sabrina by the elbow to the altar.

Sabs's headshakes ruffle her hip-length hair in an exotic pattern. Her human form is no match for Determined Catty, whose strength has multiplied with long days working on the ship. Bettina sits with wide eyes of shock throughout the exchange, belaying my worst fears—she won't be much help acclimating Sabrina to the boat. While the sisters love one another, neither has had positive experiences with the human world. How much work will it take to wedge Sabrina into my life? Wouldn't the most loving thing I could do for her is to let her go?

Sabrina's glassy, sea-green eyes implore me to rescue her, but where would I stick her? She can't live her life in my room. Even cold-hearted Magda couldn't spend her days in the captain's quarters when her vampire nature kept her indoors. It almost killed her.

Sabrina is more vibrant, but she's fragile after her ordeal. She must stay by my side at all times until she recovers. I wrap her hands around my elbow so my hands are free to handle Chub's book. Her teary expression when I nod in her direction breaks my heart. Surrounded by my mateys, with my lady love on my arm, joining my best friends in marriage is the recipe for the happiest day of my life. However, the knowledge that I'm scaring my lady half to death by dragging her on deck cuts me to ribbons. What do I do?

"Friends, Crew, me hearties…" I read Chub's scribble in the margins of the old Bible we found when we stole the boat. The words of his ceremony will be identical to what he said at Magda and Branko's wedding…at his request. As I read each solemn vow and flowery metaphor, I'm struck with gratitude. Without Chub's help, I couldn't have read the passages and would have faked it. "Do you, Catty—um, Catalina Pintarro—take this man, Quartermaster Ellis Morehouse, as your husband, to have and to hold as long as you both shall live?"

"I do," she says with love shining for my best friend.

"And do you, Quartermaster Ellis Morehouse, take Catalina Pintarro as your wife, to have and to hold as long as you both shall live?"

"Aye, with all me heart," he says, bringing their joined hands to his chest. "Catalina, I promise…"

Chub's poetic pledge of love and prosperity fades into the background. I'm captivated by the differences in our hands. My missing fingers are obvious reminders of my lurid past. Chub's beefy, stout fingers sport scars, blisters, callouses, and bruises from life on the high seas. However, he also keeps his nails impeccably clean, and the whirls of hair at his wrist are pink fuzz that speak of the educated, well-mannered man he became. Do I have a hope of assimilating into a village or island society?

Despite Catalina's money and Chub's experience in the sweet trade, there aren't wedding rings. If *Patricia's Wish* had more luck, we'd have found heaps of treasure in the five years we've sailed. A trio of incompetent captains, a plague, and countless hurricanes doomed this boat to failure. While the best days of my life were spent behind the helm or the cannon, I have nothing to show for years of work. I have my stories, but those don't buy farmland. Sabrina and I don't have two nickels to rub together.

We can't survive off the boat. She's terrified to stay on the boat.

"I love you too, Ellis," Catty wails as she throws her arms around the groom. As her lips plunder his mouth, her bouquet does its best to stab him.

Sabrina's job as maid of honor is to rescue Chub from the flowers, but she's glued to my side. I close my book of ceremonies and pry the bouquet from Catty's fingers. My lady shakes as if the storm brewing struck her with lightning. All my protective instincts flare to life. The sweet trade is not for her, but luckily, neither is village life. We are no merchant or farmer and his wife. Sabrina must be free of the human world…and I wouldn't mind shedding more of society's shackles either.

The pressure on my inner elbow changes as Sabrina shrinks a few inches. Her feet must be morphing into tentacle tips. Good thing my giant duster will cover her transformation but leave her precious soulbeak exposed for my cunning plan.

Walk the Walk

Book 5: Hooking Captain Teeth

"Get your captain some rum!" My shouts are met with cheers and whistles from the crew. The band kicks up a lively jig. Chub's fingers tap the side of his leg. One announcement, and they will dance until the heavens pour rain upon us. Let them think I'm toasting the newly married couple. I chose to enter this life when life on land was too constricting. The sweet trade's noose tightens around my neck. It's time to leave again.

"I said, someone water your captain!" My shout grows terse with urgency.

The last time I felt this certain, I stood on the gangplank of the *Queen Anne's Revenge*. The crowd's mood wavers with uncertainty as my tone gives away my inner turmoil. This is goodbye on my terms. After a healthy moment too long, Eze scrambles down the sterncastle's deck stairs.

Of course, the nutmegs would leave the helm unattended because the rest of the crew couldn't be arsed. Even Chub rolls his eyes at their incompetence. He steals Eze's flask and throws a hit down his gullet. I must take advantage of Sabrina's diverted attention and the element of surprise! His book thuds on the deck as I wrap my arm around Sabrina's shoulders and the other arm behind her knees. She squawks as I raise her to my chest.

"Catalina, would you pour, please."

"You want me to fetch a cup?" Avast ye, I forget how sheltered she is. I'd ask Chub, but I don't think Sabrina wants another man close to her delicate belly.

"A shot in my lady's naval if you please," I request. My arms tighten to metal bonds as Sabrina squirms. Catalina pours half the bottle over Sabrina's wiggling belly. Enough liquid filters through the lace panel on the jacket's front to soften her soulbeak.

"Please," she whispers, tears threatening to spill over her cheeks.

"Here's to true love," I shout as I slurp the grog from my lady's body. My teeth snap threads of silk as I root around the soulbeak. The flat of my tongue flicks it into my mouth.

Bettina wails in the crowd when she realizes what I've done. She launches herself at me, batting my shoulder with tiny fists. Catalina retreats into Chub's embrace. The crew's shouts of 'traitor' amongst the jeers and roars break my heart. They would have loved Sabrina, but I couldn't take the chance on them. If I doomed her to a life in one room, I'd never forgive myself. Wild things like Sabrina and me need space more than air.

"Fecking lot!" My shouts become scrambled cries as my mind blanks.

The pain in my knees, feet, and ankles eclipses the times I've been shot, stabbed, and burnt. I lower to the ground at half the speed of a fall as my legs divide into tentacles. Chub shouts something about removing my boots. Errant appendages thrust from my body and pound the deck, blistering the planks into splinters. The suckers along them open and close as I collect sensory information about my surroundings. I tear at my leathers hanging in tatters around my waist. When I free my gills from their clutches, I huff with renewed vigor.

Instincts stronger than I have ever known course through my veins. My tentacles slink and stalk until they meet with Sabrina's thinner tentacles. I twine them with hers, wrapping us in a ball of strength.

"We must go overboard," I say between pants, "or I'll breed you right here and now."

"Why did you choose this?" She takes my face into her hands and presses our foreheads together.

"I chose the best place for us," I reply. Her tears fall onto my cheeks. "Just because I'm determined to be with you doesn't doom you to a life of misery. I'd be a terrible husband if I didn't want to make you happy above all else. I see your struggles with humans—"

"You see me," she says, leaning back to stare into my eyes.

"Yes, Sabs, I finally see you."

"Oi! Now what! A Kraken for a captain?!" The

rude shout from the crowd earns Chub's icy glare. If he identifies them, they will boil beans for the crew and swab the poop deck the morning after.

"No, a *former* Kraken as a Captain," I shout with a chuckle. I throw Catalina's bouquet to Bettina, who fumbles it but recovers. "Long live, Captain Betts!"

"Long live, Captain Betts!" The chant rings from the ratlines above and the bilge tanks below. Fists and flasks are raised in support of Bettina's taking over the boat. Chub nods his approval before nuzzling the neck of his new wife. As much as he deserves the promotion, he's on his way out of the sweet trade and wouldn't want to be sucked back in like a whale caught in a whirlpool.

"As your Captain, I now pronounce both couples—husbands and wives! You may now kiss your brides!" Bettina's shouts are accompanied by a frenzy of cheers. She pumps the bouquet over her head like a champion sword, and the crew rallies for a battle.

Chub wastes no time in bending Catalina into a low dip and kissing her senselessly.

"Wives—plural?" Sabrina murmurs.

"Married like a proper couple," Bettina scolds, wagging the bouquet at her sister. "I know you two, and you'll have eggs by nightfall. My little nieces and nephews must be legitimate, born from holy matrimony…well, as holy as you whores can be."

Walk the Walk

Book 5: Hooking Captain Teeth

"Then I'll kiss my bride." I grab Sabrina's chin to turn her stare from her sister to me. My lips claim hers as my tongue spears her mouth. A fire ignites between us. My tentacles squeeze her as our new appendages writhe against one another. Three pockets open at my waistline. Out of the central one pops my new Kraken cock. I can't wait to learn all the ways to quiff my wife in my new body.

"Teeth, we need the water," Sabrina whines against my lips.

"I can think of something I need more," I growl against her lips.

"Captain," Chub yells over our heads. Catty smothers a giggle behind her hand as Chub laughs out loud at us. "Permission to throw the Kraken whores overboard for indecency."

"Permission granted," Bettina yells with a broad smile stretching her cheeks. Her giggle brings tears to my lady's eyes.

I shelter Sabs in my arms as the crew hoists us into the air. She tucks her head in her arms and leans into my body as dozens of hands clutch our bodies. I guess we're taking my dusters and best dress shirt with us into the abyss. The crew sings a bawdy song about a man lured to his death by a siren who dies with a smile on his lips. I laugh at the audacity.

"One for the boat!" They yell as they swing us

over the edge and back.

"Two for her crew! Three pays what's due!" We swing twice more. Sabrina shrieks each time we sail back onto the boat.

"And four in hopes you float!"

My laughter trails down the Jacob's ladder as we fly over the railing and into the drink. The ocean smacks my back. Sabrina fights out of my embrace as soon as we are enveloped in seawater. I chose the Kraken form not only to accommodate her fear of humans but also to explore life under the sea. In my mind, I concocted adventures we would take together. She slides through my tentacles and disappears in a cloud of ink as soon as we touch the sand.

Did I make a mistake?

Chapter

15

Sabrina

"No, no, no," I scream at the lemon sharks gathering above us. Teeth just sprouted tentacles. He's not ready to fight off a shiver of lemon sharks—despite how much he calls his enemies "yellow bellies." I don't know if he's figured out his gills, siphon, or beak. My heart tears in two. He could die before we get the chance to start our lives together.

Where should I focus? Stay with him and teach him how to use his Kraken body, or fight off the growing threat above us? If any of his hearties jump in after us for a post-ceremony bath, sharks will swarm them. The devastation of luring his friends to their deaths by deciding to be a Kraken for me would tear him apart. His bitterness would tear us apart. As much as it will hurt him, I must abandon him to fight off the sharks. He will figure out his new body…

…oh no, my empty-headed husband isn't the best at figuring out…anything.

Too late. I release a cloud of black ink over Teeth to hide him from the sharks. Hopefully, he has enough time to learn how to breathe underwater before he suffocates. Without knowing how to control his siphon, he will stay anchored on the bottom of the sea—much too deep for lemon sharks to dive. His gigantic tentacles will walk him across the sandy bottom, but even they don't have the heft to lift such a large Kraken. But when he learns to control his new body, he will be a force of nature.

There are ten lemon sharks, with more golden shadows in the distance. The most curious one will approach me in three…two… *Punch!* I hit the shark's sensitive nose with an uppercut. The animal rolls onto his back, which momentarily stuns him. As he floats to shallower water, the tides will turn him over, and he will swim off as if nothing happened. There's no reason to kill these scallywags—they are more of a nuisance to the born Kraken than anything else. More importantly, they are food for the tiger sharks, who are a real threat to us.

A shark's body brushes my lower back as it swims daringly close.

I punch two more lemon sharks—one with my fist and his friend with one of my tentacles. I must keep two tentacles by my side for punching and the other six cycling beneath me to keep me afloat. Spinning, I keep the closest shark in view. If I lead this battle to Teeth, he would be caught in the fray unarmed. Whirling around, I punch another shark. Bodies float around me as if I've stunk the water. I dodge them to assess the angle of the next shark. Damn shark curiosity makes them worse than alley cats. Where are they? A shiver of six circles above. Four lay stunned.

Two sharks bump their bodies against the tentacles to my left.

Ouch! Pain blooms from the tip of my right propulsion tentacle. Bastard nipped me! Worse than the toothmark scarring the smooth, red appendage, a fist-sized cloud of blood releases. The six circling change their swim pattern to include shallow dives as they smell the blood. What was a steady onslaught of curious animals changes into a feeding frenzy.

We aren't safe here. Lemon sharks are cannibals, and their bloodshed will attract bigger predators. While lemon sharks can't reach Teeth on the bottom, what they attract might have a deeper dive. What do I do? I could outswim them and retreat to deeper waters if I were alone. Teeth's bulk was my strength limit in his human form. Carrying his Kraken form? I don't have a prayer. I doubt I could push him across the bottom. There's no time to plan. Hopefully, those nutmegs aboard the ship notice the splashing sharks and stay out of the water. Human sacrifices are the last thing I need.

I dodge a large lemon shark who snaps one of the stunned sharks in half. The blood cloud tints the sea red. I twist to avoid the cloud touching me and collide with a smaller lemon shark. *Ouch!* The bastard bites my elbow. I punch its nose. As the body floats upward, it's swallowed whole by a tiger shark.

The stripes of a tiger shark send shivers down the tentacles of any Kraken—let alone a small one like me, surrounded by other predators.

My body contorts into a myriad of shapes to avoid teasing bites from the smaller lemon sharks. They love the consortium of tiny octopi and crustaceans in the coastal reefs. I don't blame them for testing an animal that smells like their favorite food. I'm much too big for them to eat, but if I were injured, they might hope for a limb to fill their bellies. The more blood they spill, the more sharks they will attract.

A tiger shark's bite would be fatal.

Should I blow another cloud of ink to shield Teeth? Teeth? Where the hell did he go? He should be where I left him on the bottom. Did he drown and float to the surface while I bungled this shark attack?

The tiger shark bears down on me at full speed—too fast to dive. If I drop to the bottom, it will swim over me…heading for where I left Teeth on the return pass…or leaving it free to breach the surface and gobble a floating Teeth. I'm paralyzed with indecision. My tentacles shrink into a ball to protect my beak…as if I carry eggs.

I'll never carry eggs! My first day as a wife, and I'm eaten by—

A navy blue tentacle, the width of my waist, flashes before my eyes. It wraps around the tiger shark and squeezes. The animal bursts into a shower of blood, guts, and fins. Lemon sharks abandon their examination of my tiny wounds for a better scent. They descend upon the floating guts in a feeding frenzy. Larger lemon sharks, dissatisfied by the size of the tiger shark bites, hunt their brethren. Are those new blood clouds from snapped lemon sharks or further leakage from the tiger shark?

A pair of giant blue tentacles wrap around my waist and haul me backward. I hit Teeth's chest with a thud. His arms cross over my clavicle as he hugs me against him. Warmth surrounds me in a loving embrace. With a torrent of bubbles, we sail through the water.

"Tell me where to swim," he orders. The authority in his voice, laced with the thrill of his rescue, sends shivers through my body. "I'm not so stupid as to remain in blood-stained water, but I'm more lost than a nun in a brothel. Bloody ocean looks the same no matter which way I face."

"To deeper water," I reply, pointing to the south. "Stay as close to the sandy bottom as you can with your—"

"Impressively massive, monster tentacles," he interrupts with joy and pride coating his words. "Don't worry, my lady, I'll keep you safe."

"I believe you," I whisper, and shockingly, I do. My vicious pirate nuzzles my neck like he did on land, and I'm reminded he's fought to survive most of his life. He rose to Captain without the brains for the job. His battle skills and charisma won the votes.

A shark frenzy isn't the worst threat in the ocean, but this one nearly overwhelmed me. Panic is what kills most Kraken…that and humans. Teeth must learn about fishing nets and hooks trolling through the water. Yes, he bested those sharks by assessing the threat correctly. But does he know that smiling dolphins are ten times more vicious? How will he react to an orca who is his size? Instead of terrified, I'm excited by everything I get to teach him.

We will be okay.

I snuggle into his arms until we reach the center of the Caribbean Sea. The journey that takes me half a day Teeth swims in a few hours—whilst holding me, and against a building current. His tentacles dance beneath us in an unorthodox pattern. I can't wait to experience the rush of soaring through the water when he learns to swim properly. Wait…what about when he learns to use his siphon to propel us?

Wow…my mate is…wow.

"Let's rest on the flat rock," I say, pointing to a plateau surrounded by deep blue water. He must be tired. He's using limbs he didn't own when he awoke. Yes, the rock is in the open, but watching for predators is key until Teeth learns his tentacles.

He barrel rolls us to the rock in a flurry of bubbles. I can't help the squeal that escapes my lips. Rocks and coral grow at an alarming rate as we approach the bottom of the sea. His answering chuckle as we settle is music to my ears. How can Teeth be cheerful and playful? I forgot how infectious his bright moods can be.

"We're lying in Davey Jones's Locker without dying," he says between belly-quaking laughter. "Kinda worrisome considering how many men I've sent here…or threatened to send here."

"What are you expecting? A hoard of disgruntled dead pirates?"

"Exactly," he replies, hair tickling my body as his nod waves it around. "We say dead men tell no tales, but I think that rule changes when you join them at the bottom of the Caribbean Sea."

"I've lived my entire life down here and never seen a pirate," I say, stifling my own laughter. "I think you're safe."

The warm rock on my back is a comfort after the narrow escape from danger. Our tentacles tangle as they drape over the end of the rock. Tucked against his side, I sigh with contentment. His bicep is more supportive than the firmest feather pillow. The other arm across my ribs hasn't let go since we fled the sharks.

I'm safe in his care.

"So, we got the learning about sharks lesson out of the way," he says with a lop-sided smirk. "What do Kraken do for fun?"

"Harass ships," I say with a laugh. He tugs his beard as he contemplates all the pranks he could pull on a ship…but let's see how many he recognizes. "My hobbies are stealing anchors, bending rudders, snipping Jacob's ladders from boat hulls, stealing fish off hooks, and wreaking havoc on bathing day."

"You little minx," he growls before pouncing on me. His fingers tickle my gills as he bites my throat with teasing nips. I'm laughing too hard for us to kiss properly, so we bang our teeth as he plunders my mouth. "Your revenge on me messed with me hearties for years, didn't it?"

"I admit nothing," I reply with wide, innocent eyes.

"Everything I learn about you makes me love

you more."

"You love me?"

"Of course," he says, reclining on the rock. I don't know what to say. He's so casual. I've waited years for him to love me as I loved him at first sight. This is more special because he wasn't born with a soulbond waiting to be fulfilled. He chose to be mine.

"I love you too…and not just for completing the soulbond…and choosing for us to live as Krakens." He deserves to know the truth—I would choose his adventurous heart without the soulbond.

"I was growing tired of the sweet trade. Chub called it ennui."

"I don't know what that is." He takes my hand, lacing our fingers together to mirror the loose tangles of our tentacles.

"It's a sickness caused by loneliness and boredom," he says with a sigh. "You saved me. I was alone on a boat filled with family."

Schools of fish flee for cover from the oncoming storm, but luckily, none are larger than my fist. Sand kicks up to the west. I haven't a moment to enjoy my new life with Teeth before his brow scrunches with concern.

"Their first night under a new captain, and it's a hurricane," he murmurs.

"Will Bettina be okay?" My heart jumps into my

throat.

"Chub will tie her to a mast if he doesn't lock her below deck with Catty. That little troll is protective to a fault."

"I doubt my sister will hide below deck."

"No," he replies. "She refused to when we took that Spanish prize, which was scarier than a hurricane. A hurricane resembles the wind and rain we battle every week until it sweeps you overboard or tears your hull to bits."

"We can swim alongside the boat and catch anyone who flies overboard. I've done that before," I whisper. He stops petting my belly to roll toward me. Recognition flares in his eyes. "Yes, Teeth, I've saved you, Chub, Eze, Greenhorn, and most of the nutmegs who fly off your boat."

"If I didn't love you before, I'd be smitten now. Thank you for saving my family."

"I'm sorry to take you away from them."

"Oh, Sabs, I chose this life. I chose you," he says, squeezing me closer.

"Why? I could have followed the boat or met you at agreed-upon island taverns on the full moons." I rub slow circles over his heart.

He's the same Teeth, but different at the same time. His chest hair is gone. The hair on his head has thicker strands that shine like spun gold. His namesake teeth are jagged points instead of blunt, human teeth. Despite the newly ferocious smile, his cocky, lop-sided grin is exactly the same.

"Sabs, love, I'd bet my front teeth that you'd never step foot in a tavern again. If me hearty crew was too much, a room of drunken strangers would scare you to death."

"You noticed? I tried my best to hold it together." My cheeks burn like the fires of hell. I bet they are as red as my tentacles.

"Chub noticed—" Teeth pauses to chuckle when I groan and cover my face "—but he notices everything. That's why I left the ship in Bettina's care. He will notice her strengths and weaknesses and train her to work around them. She will be easier to teach than me."

"Maybe it was difficult for you because you were in the wrong skin."

"What do you mean?" His confused expression is too handsome for words. I kiss it from his features before I can stop myself.

"You took to using gills and tentacles within minutes. I assumed I would have to teach you like a newborn hatchling."

"Hatchling?"

"Yes," I say as my fiery blush creeps down my neck and into his duster. My nipples harden against the rough lace and smooth leather. The contrasting sensations against them are maddening. "I lay eggs in this form, and Teeth, I want lots and lots of eggs."

Chapter 16

Teeth

"Now, there's a lesson! How do I quiff with a cock trapped in my bilge?"

Her laughter echoes in the empty sea. The tone is muffled, deeper, and somehow sweeter than she sounds on land. Her carefree attitude is worth the loss of my life as a pirate. I hope I never see the haunted look in her eyes, hinting that she's nothing more than a hollow shell of herself, again. My vibrant Sabrina is restored. The best part is I have a new landscape to learn—where I'm one of the few sentient species.

No more *Dumb Teeth* hiding behind bravado.

"Stop clawing at your belly," Sabrina says, gliding on top of me. She holds my wrists against my pelvic bone, and I'll be damned if a pocket opens below my naval. "Your charms hide in your abdomen, pirate."

"There's a subject where I don't need help. Every pirate finds his cock on his maiden voyage at least once," I quip to earn her giggle.

I'm captivated by her exotic beauty. Her wild hair floats around her head as the current moves like a wind that blows just for her. Sparkling, sea-green eyes narrow with desire. Her plump lips open slightly to taste the water around us. I wear the same expression as I intoxicate myself with her arousal permeating the water. It flows through my lips, nostrils, and gills to focus every organ in my new body on breeding her. Everywhere her slender fingers touch me burns.

My new instincts cloud my human thoughts. I don't care how we will conceive, birth, or parent hatchlings—only the need to give them to her rippling beneath my skin matters. It's on the tip of my tongue to tell her when her eyes flutter closed, and I lose the connection. She's a gorgeous monster leaning toward my tender underbelly. The hairs on the back of my neck stand on end as my mind spins with images of Sabs biting through my intestines, kissing her way between my tentacles, or…

Avast ye! Her tiny tongue swirling around the pocket in my pelvis pulls a groan from the deepest parts of me. She teases the creases with her fingertips while that tongue flicks, licks, and penetrates me. Pressure builds. Fire races up my spine. A sensation akin to spilling overwhelms my nerves as my cock extrudes through the pocket. Twice the girth and a few extra inches in length make my Kraken cock a monster befitting my lady.

Goodbye human body! I'll never miss you now!

"Bloody hell, Sabs, that felt incredible," I pant as I push my new marriage rod as far out of my pouch as I can.

"We're just getting started," she replies with a giggle. She bends backward to lift her hips off me. With rapt attention, I salivate over the slit opening in her pelvis. It shines with thicker cream than the seawater surrounding us.

"You want me," I whisper as she rolls her eyes.

I grab her narrow hips and pull her treasure box toward my hungry mouth. When she resists, my tentacles push her forward. My new strength not only puffs my chest with pride but thrills my mate, who rewards my aggression all over my chin. I feast on her slit. She's quiet, and I struggle to remember if she was a quiet lover as a human. Squeezed eyes, bitten lower lip, and fingers tangled in my hair, my mate holds me to her. When I spear her with my tongue, her hips thrust subconsciously.

My new favorite vision is my mate lost in pleasure.

Lost in a forest of her hip-length hair, I wait for her shuddering to wane. The tremors of her climax rattle my chin and suck my tongue deeper into her body. I nuzzle my nose at the apex of the opening to trigger her delicate gasps. She pulls my hair so hard, I bet she will return to earth with handfuls released from my scalp.

Like a sweet ragdoll, she collapses against my chest. My cock wedges in the notch between two of her tentacles. She brushes and teases my sugarstick, rolling it between the appendages. The pressure and lazy tempo aren't enough to inspire my spend but drive me mad with arousal. As she cools her feverish body, I thrust upward and take on her heat. The motion releases some of the tension at the base of my spine, but I'm helplessly seeking pleasure from the tide. My tip is too cold in the open water while my shaft burns with pent-up desire.

"You torture me, wife," I whisper.

"Good," she says as she plants tiny kisses along my jaw. "I'll erase the memory of every strumpet who's sweetened your sugarstick. Replace their faces in your mind with writhing tentacles using pleasure beyond your wildest dreams. Wait until animal instincts push your human sensibilities out of your consciousness."

Walk the Walk

Book 5: Hooking Captain Teeth

Sabrina

"My dear wife," he says with a chuckle that betrays how calm and ordered his thoughts rest. "You are sweet if you think that I have any sensibilities."

The pressure of wedding an experienced lover could fill the deepest ocean trench. My only advantage is the growing love between us. He saves me. I comfort and teach him. We have everything in line for the perfect partnership promised by a soulbond. I just need to believe in it. I don't need a whore's techniques when I have the love of a wife.

With renewed confidence, I dislodge his cock from my tentacles grip. I try to slink down his body with grace, but the churning current kicks up sand around us. A halo of gold surrounds him. I'm coughing and wheezing as it clogs my gills and irritates my face. His rough thumbs caress my eyelids as he rubs the sand from my eyes. Despite the interruption to my seduction, I continue my momentum with his pre-fluid painting a line up my belly.

I hover over his purple tip and lick my lips.

Walk the Walk

Book 5: Hooking Captain Teeth

Shimmying my shoulders, I wedge my breasts in the joints of his tentacles. He responds with light pulses of the tentacle muscles to work my flesh. I reward him with a swipe of my tongue over his slit. The cloud of fluid he releases replaces the sand in my face with an arousal-inducing scent. My control slips a touch, and my plan to seduce him falls to the bottom of the sea. I engulf his member in one gulp, swallowing as he hits the back of my throat.

Suction hollows my cheeks. The flap between my nose and mouth seals tightly. I only breathe through my gills, so I can pleasure him longer than a human. My scalp tingles as he tentatively threads his fingers through my hair. He shakes with the struggle to hold back and treat me respectfully.

That will never do.

I lash the sensitive underside of his root with my tongue in brutal strokes while strangling his tip with my throat muscles. Trained by swallowing fish whole since I was a hatchling, my muscles match the rhythmic pulses of a woman in climax. My fingers squeeze his against my head to demonstrate my permission to use me. The rumbling growl from his chest has me lifting my gaze to check on him.

His pained snarl lights a fire in my slit. I want him…badly.

I grin with the power I have over the largest

Kraken I've ever seen. The expression is pushed from my features as his control snaps. My nose presses against his pubic bone as he grinds. Cold saltwater lifts goose-pimples on my cheeks when he withdraws. An obstinate pout traps my prize in my mouth. He holds me, perched on the tip, whimpering for his next thrust.

My lips burn as he shoves through the opening toward the back of my throat. Over and over, they glide over his flesh. His grunts and growls are music to my ears. I clutch two of his tentacles to stop myself from fingering into my slit. He coils his tentacles around my wrists and tentacles. I'm stretched flat over him, his taste flooding my senses. Heat from his body battles with the dropping temperature of the water, keeping me on edge. His shaft pulses twice, and I bite the base gently. When I release my teeth, he releases his seed down my throat.

His hands fall to the rock with a thud. His tentacles disturb the sand as they plop lifelessly to the bottom. I lay my head on his hip, resting my cheek on the bone. My tongue flicks his softened shaft to coax it back to life. Each touch sends a jolt through his body, tensing his arms and quivering his gills next to my temple.

"Give me a second, love."

"Not in a thousand years," I growl. My licks progress to the sensitive underside of his tip.

"That's my wife. Blimey, how am I ready to go again?"

"Mating fluids in my slit harden you, and you chugged them faster than a tankard of grog. I must be careful not to release too much—"

"Or what?"

I hesitate a heartbeat, long enough he raises an eyebrow at me.

"Your cock detaches."

"Forever?"

I laugh because the horror on his face always gives me the giggles.

"It regenerates—"

"You could collect them and stuff them—"

"Don't even think about it," I reply, dropping my forehead onto him as I continue to laugh. "The seawater decomposes them faster than you can grow another one."

"Blimey, my cock as fish food isn't an image I ever want to see in real life."

His candid confession pulls even richer laughter from the depths of my soul. This is the emotional piece our relationship never had on land. The joy, banter, and stolen moments of friends as well as lovers. It's hotter than the magical things he does with his fingers.

"Stop teasing me, Sabs," he says with a jarring seriousness. "How do I give you the eggs you want?"

"The more you seed my womb, the more eggs will mature into hatchlings. I'll lay them in less than a moon cycle…and then we get to start the process all over again."

"We don't raise them? How are you so close to Bettina if you don't grow up in families?" I love how his face is twisted with questions and not judgment.

"Parents abandon the egg clutch to the will of the sea. Bettina and I were in the same egg clutch," I answer. "We're close because we raised one another. When we visit the Atlantic Ocean in the winter, you will meet who I think is my father. His red hair, green eyes, and red tentacles are identical to Bettina's and mine. Does the lack of parenting bother you?"

"My father abandoned us. My mother did her best but…sold her sons to merchants as cabin boys. We went into the sweet trade on different boats to escape the brutality of *decent men*. My mother also sold my sister, Melanie, to a brothel. Little Melanie *worked* herself to death before the age of sixteen. Blimey, I'd rather my children raise themselves than mess them up like my parents did me." His frown seems to pull down his whole being instead of just the corners of his mouth.

"You don't seem messed up to me," I say to soothe him.

"Because I found the correct skin for this world,"

he says with a bittersweet smile that hides his teeth. "Nothing more complicated than animals fighting to survive and procreate— Wait, you turn human every full moon—"

"Not anymore," I interrupt with my hand over his mouth. "Our hatchlings may if their soulbond is tethered to land, but those bonds are none of our business."

"All the conception but none of the responsibility?"

"It's not all bad being a Kraken," I whisper as I slide up his body. He bows his head to capture my mouth. I open immediately to accept his claim over me. The heaviness of our conversation has done nothing to cool my libido. If anything, he stroked the flames higher with his honest questions and revealed secrets.

"Nothing with you could be bad," he says against my lips.

I bring our tangled tentacles into a ball beneath us. My tentacle tip teases the beak between his. I suck in seawater to rinse my slit and blow it over his engorged cock. Oh, the noises he makes twist my insides into a needy mess.

"Please," I whine when his tentacle teases my beaked entrance in return.

"I'll quiff you every way possible. Nothing is

off-limits," he says between labored breaths. His gills contract and release under my fingertips like little mouths. "Teach me to love you, Sabrina."

He steals the words from my mouth with a gruff penetration of his tentacle into my beak. It wiggles, withdraws, and punches inside of me with brutal strokes. I return the favor as our tentacles form a writhing coil. Their momentum lifts us from the rock and sits us upright. Suspended in the current, we sway and drift with the building seas.

But who cares when he rolls my nipples with the decadent tugs I love?

"Like this?" He asks with his tip notched at my slit's entrance.

"Just like on the beach," I whine between cries. With infinite tenderness, he slides into my waiting siphon slit. We lock together as only destined mates can—bound together body to body, heart to heart, and soul to soul with loving ties.

His tentacle wedges itself higher than I have dared to stick anything up that orifice. I'm skewered on him like a marionette on her master's stick. I wail as it curves in wicked strokes toward my inner walls as if seeking dark pleasure points.

He shoves a second tentacle in my mouth.

My eyes roll back in bliss as I suck him into my throat. As long as he doesn't try to quiff my gills, I can breathe…

I may die from pleasure anyway.

Our bodies rub and writhe as we work ourselves into a frenzy. I'm climaxing and over-stimulated within minutes, while my experienced husband works my body to wring every last drop of excitement from me. His growls turn to grunts as his smooth thrusts lose their rhythm. Each jerk sprays my slit with seed.

My womb opens and closes like a beached fish's mouth to gulp his gift. The rolling of dormant eggs in my abdomen shifts my orgasms to a deeper location in my body, giving my poor pleasure button on my slit's opening a rest. A heaviness settles inside me as each egg receives Teeth's love. The sensation combined with Teeth's torture of my nipples blends my orgasms into a never-ending plea for more.

We spin and tumble through the Caribbean as a mass of writhing tentacles. Our opposing colors are the only clue we are two individuals and not one giant animal. My cries time themselves to ring between his grunts until he sucks one of my tentacles into his mouth. The scrape of his teeth zeros my focus onto his handsome face. My palms hold his cheeks as he seeds me repeatedly. We don't break our gazes until we're limp with exhaustion.

I flop uselessly in his arms as he lowers us to the sea floor. His tentacles instinctively burrow into the sand to evict any sand fleas or larger irritants. Satisfied we won't wake with welts, he buries our lower halves. With tenderness I've never seen him use, he arranges my upper body and fans my hair on the bottom. His affectionate caresses as he covers my arms and shoulders with camouflaging sand bring tears to the corners of my eyes.

"Rest, my wife," he says with a whisper of a kiss. He smooths the hair over my brow one last time before burying his belly and arms.

"I can feel our eggs," I whisper when they shift and roll in my still body.

"Do they make you happy?"

"Yes, I love you so much."

"Good," he says with a sexy drowsiness in his voice. "Then my work is done."

"What about the hurricane?"

"Rest first. Kisses second. Hurricane third," he replies with a yawn. "Captain's orders."

Walk the Walk

Book 5: Hooking Captain Teeth

Thirsty for more of the crew on Patricia's Wish? We weigh anchor again…but this time, Captain Betts steers the ship.

Bettina

With Quartermaster Chub and his wife's counsel, I've settled into my role as a pirate queen like a guppy to the sea. I don't miss my Kraken tentacles now that I have a purpose. This crew of rag-tag misfits depends on me to keep them afloat, fed, and not swinging from a Sheriff's picture frame. Our first trip up the eastern coast of the continental colonies is honest work, but that doesn't mean a prize won't turn our heads toward the sweet trade. Once I offload the debauched satyr we're removing from Boston's high society, our crew will seek our fortunes.

Hybris

When my parents named me, they shouldn't have picked the word for overconfidence, willful arrogance, or insubordination. All I did was live up to their expectations. It's not like I steal, fistfight, or murder. I'm a lover, not a fighter…which is exactly why I've been exiled from Boston. If those women prized their virginity more, they wouldn't have begged me to relieve them of it. Oh, their pretty pleas ring in my ears as my parents lecture on my responsibilities in civilized society! My ruined reputation isn't my fault, but who listens to an *other*? As I board the ship, I can't prove my parents hired pirates to make me disappear, but it's my gut feeling.

Hybris triggers everything in Bettina's painful past, but she can't behead him as promised in her contract with his parents. The ship seems to shrink as he befriends the crew and worms his way closer to her. What will she do with the salacious satyr? Certainly not fall for his charming ways… Find out in *Shiver Me Satyr* as part of the Time for Monsters series in 2025.

Walk the Walk

Book 5: Hooking Captain Teeth

Bonus Content from Walk the Plank by Marilyn Barr

Did Chub and Teeth really sail under a vampiress or were they puffing their feathers like roosters? Believe it or not, this is one fish tale the mischievous pair didn't stretch from mast to mast. Read how Blackbeard marooned them, how they escaped colonial Carolina, and stole *Patricia's Wish* from under the British soldiers' noses in Walk the Walk Book 1: Walk the Plank. Here's a special sneak peek!

Branko, former Captain of Patricia's Wish

"Why did we act like a bunch of ninnies? We should have ganged together and hung the old demon by his gingamobs!"

Who's passing on the other side of the trees? I unsheathe my dagger by reflex. As long as Magda is tucked in her pyramid, she is camouflaged. However, I've left my pratts where anyone can find them. At most, there are thirty yards of trees between our camp

Walk the Walk

Book 5: Hooking Captain Teeth

and the ocean. I have less than five minutes to formulate a plan before they trample on us. Picking them off one-by-one would be ideal but there isn't the time or distance to do so. Am I outnumbered? How long do I have until sunset? If I can hold them off, Magda's fangs would double my fighting power...if she would have the nutmegs to fight... Blimey, I have a lot of ifs...

"Not me!" barks a second voice through the trees. "I've been his Nimgimmer for weeks and his balls are rotted with pox. I wouldn't touch him again—even to hang him by 'em."

I'd know this second voice anywhere. Snips, the ship's doctor from the *QAR*, is within these trees. In our early days, his primary job was stitching us up after battles. He got his name from the way he yanked the floss to tie a final knot before cutting any excess thread. We would bellow for him to get the scissors or snips without the final tug. However, in the last few weeks, his job has been being the crew's venereal disease doctor. If he jumped ship because he was sick of looking at pimply cocks all day, I wouldn't blame him.

The sky has an apricot tint, but too many rays remain to wake Magda. I will have to face the intruders to protect her. Who is with Snips, and who do they wish to hang? Were they sent to find me? I scatter the remnants of last night's ashes with my boot and creep to the base of the largest tree in our circle. There are at least four pairs of rustling bushes. Whoever accompanies Snips doesn't understand stealth, or this is a large group. A knot forms in my stomach as I picture myself ambushing me hearties.

"We should have shown that bilge-sucker the black spot while we had the chance—" The way Chub draws out his vowels is unmistakable. The Irishman claims to be from England, but his brogue gives him away whenever he opens his mouth. His temper must be pricked for his accent to go unchecked. To roll his vowels and threaten Blackbeard with mutiny in the same sentence is bad business…unless you are on the run from said Captain…

"Yeah, serve him a black spot with Willie Mace sharpening his knives over the demon's shoulder? I'd rather be keelhauled under the *QAR* than get on his bad side. He carves for fun, and I'm not talking about whittling." Only Teeth has such a fear of William Mace. Perhaps it is because he has a pretty face which he would like to keep or because he has more brains than the lot of us cast together. William has been known to give up his share of the booty in return for a prisoner to have at his disposal. Anyone who's mopped his room knows he consumed them, not just killed 'em.

The more I weave around the trees, the more my

spirits climb. Each comment I gather from the group points toward us being of equal mind. If only the trees had horizontal branches, I could gain the high ground. From that vantage point, I could shout down to them and gauge their footing without getting shot. This unforgiving terrain has minimal bushes and no canopy for hiding. Still, the hope of joining me hearties pushes me onward.

"Someone needs to hunt the scurvy dog after what's he's done to us. I'd elect Black Sparta, but he vanished after Branko jumped ship. If anyone can cleave the old captain to brisket, Branko or Black Sparta would be my pick." This voice is definitely Boom, the cannon master of the *QAR*. And Boom is never without Sharp, the taciturn weapon's steward. Where is the vessel if the crew marooned their doctor, cannon master, weapon's steward, and two senior hands?

"Good riddance to the lotta 'em. All those flowery words and we fell for them like virginal brides. I'm too old for their gobshite. All I asked was to die on the high seas with a full belly and an empty cock. Bastards denied me all three, and for what? Fear of mutiny. We hid behind Edward Teach— yes, I'm calling him by his name, not some moniker born from madness. He's simply a man, not a demon, but was willing to play one. We believed his lies because they suited us until our presence didn't suit him. Where does that leave us? Carolina. Godforsaken Carolina with no letters of marquee, governors' letters of pardon, or demon to scare off the local law enforcement."

The crotchety old voice can only be Bud. Bud earned his name with his ability to detect real gold from fake by taste. He bites coins to verify them, but also carries a special monocle to see inside gems. One look and he can spot fake stones and the real thing. Grouchy bastard wouldn't teach me or anyone else his trade, either. Claims he's stayed alive as long as he has because he can't be replaced. Due to his yellow belly and habit of hiding when we board treasure vessels, he's wise to hoard his skills.

His speech motivates my feet. These men were swindled like me. We could band together and reclaim the vessel. We could steal another sea rover together and go back to the sweet trade. In the least, they may know a boat heading to Nassau. My prospects have gone from zero to infinite. I trample plants and swat at branches as I fight toward my friends. Their grumbles grow louder. I'm almost upon them when my brain stutters. What about Magda?

I'm pondering my relationship with Sea Hag when I collide with Sharp. He growls and pushes me on instinct. I ricochet off Bud and plow over Chub before landing on my arse. Sharp has his shooter drawn before I can draw a breath. The barrel is aimed between my eyes. "Avast, ye scoundrel! I will shoot a third eye socket in ye skull!"

"It's me, you pudding-headed fellow," I say while dusting the vegetation from my sleeves. My eyes stick to the task so that I won't reveal my terror at being held at gunpoint by the fastest shooter on the *QAR*. Lady luck must be watching over me for him to ask first and shoot later. His habit is the reverse.

"Branko, as I live and breathe!" Chub says as he rolls to my side. I'm not comforted by having him so close. The guy is chest-height on me, but can lift more cargo than all of us put together. His short stature hides that he's strong as an ox and as mean as one, as well.

"I'm as surprised to see you," I tell him from my spot on the ground. Talking to these men after fleeing the boat is like holding a loaded cannon before the order to fire. I give up the high ground to show them I'm not interested in taking on the six of them. "What happened? Why aren't you sailing?"

"We were marooned by Blackbeard," Sharp says while tucking in his gun. A bead of sweat drips down my spine as the pistol slides into its holster. "Bastard beached the *QAR* ashore just there"—he pauses to gesture eastward, "punctured all but one dingy, and took the good one to *The Adventure*. All planned, it was. The vessel was waiting just off our starboard for him to climb jacob's ladder. Never seen anything so cowardly in my life."

I'm shocked. The invincible Blackbeard not only abandoned his ship for a smaller one in his fleet but also removed the means for his crew to follow him. Why didn't he fire everyone legitimately? Has his mysterious illness gone to his brain? I try to put myself in Blackbeard's place and see his logic. He trades a large boat for a smaller one…one unable to attack a naval vessel… Ooooh, a smaller boat could navigate the narrow passages of the barrier islands along the coast. He must hope to hide in the territory of the Carolina Governor, amongst the sandbars and coastal villages. This radically changes my plans.

"Like rats fleeing a sinking ship," Chub adds on.

"Was Black Sparta with him?"

"Nope, I will correct myself. He was like *a rat* fleeing a sinking ship. Haven't seen Sparta since you vanished. We reckoned you split together," Chub answers.

"Ye hearties were angry at you for leaving. Then, we were angry at Captain because William Mace let slip you were to be traded for quicksilver in port. I'm afraid you have made a dangerous enemy," Bud says before offering his hand to Chub to help him stand. I jump to my feet using my special abilities. Bud offers me a sly smile.

"Mace is on *The Adventure*, right? He was promoted to being the vessel's captain last summer over Black Sparta—after Mace served on the QAR under Sparta for a season too."

"Kicked your man in the pratts when Blackbeard chose Mace over him. We should have seen the change in tides from that choice," says Snips. He punctuates his statement with a load of spit sent behind him. Teeth jumps out of the way at the last second and shoots a glare to the good doctor. "Sparta's not with you or he'd have killed us all for our first collision. Whatcha doing in Cape Fear when we left you in Charles Town? Obviously not much if you're wandering the trees without more than your duffle."

"I'm crossing the rice paddies to Bath, where I'm taking my own ship. I thought to avoid Cape Fear in case the Sheriff's picture frame waits to hang me. Governor owns my head for his plantation. I had my skin sold from my back, but I won't go without a fight." Each man swallows his pride when I reveal our Captain's plan. Chub, Snips, and Teeth are exempt from such treachery due to their bright, white skin. Boom, Sharp, and Bud are the same color as me. Sharp joined the *QAR* from the same slave ship raid that rescued me. We liberated Boom later that same Summer.

I'm watching Snips for a response, but Boom takes the leadership position. "Do you have a crew?"

"Do you see me hearties here to save my arse from you lot?"

"We joined together in freedom. We die for freedom, but in between, we have the freedom to choose to work together." Bud started our crewman's pledge, but we've all been reciting the words by the end. Hugs are exchanged, and my spirit soars.

"Well, isn't this a touching sight?"

My blood runs cold at the frigid tone of her voice. I lost track of the sun's descent. My she-devil has awoken to find me swearing allegiance to strangers. Strangers to her, at least. I must do some heavy damage control.

I flash my most flirtatious smile and hope she falls for it. "Happy to see ya, darling."

Her brows lower into angry slashes. "Branko, why don't you introduce me to your friends? Are they coming with us?"

"Oh no, lady," Chub stammers with waving hands in front of his person. "We do not sail on a boat carrying a lady."

"Tis bad luck," echoes Boom.

"Sorry, old boy, but if your offer is to sail with her, we are out!" Snips claps my shoulder before stepping away. The others shift to follow him with my hopes of safely traveling with a band of men. I hadn't realized how precarious my situation was with Magda until given the option of surrounding myself with allies.

"Wait—" I sound a little more desperate than I wish, but sailing a vessel with a known crew is a sailor's dream. I hoped to recruit a skeleton crew in Bath to trade for passage to Nassau, but they would be wildcards who could slit my throat in my sleep. Of course, Magda is a wildcard herself. Sailing alone with her is more than I can handle, too. One of us would have to steer while the other…did everything else. What I could have flashes before my eyes now—a crew of my own. "We worked like clockwork for Blackbeard. Don't you want those voyages for ourselves?"

"How dare you abandon Branko because of me?!" Magda screeches. "You don't know me and what I'd bring to a crew!" She stomps her foot and splashes Snips to his knees, earning her a deeper scowl.

If she's trying to win over the men by proving she's a lady pirate, she just blew it. Chub's eyebrows climb his forehead. Sharp bares his false metal teeth. Bud chuckles and waves a dismissive hand at her. She fumes in return with her fists clenched and her lips pressed together. I can practically smell the smoke coming from her ears. Perhaps choosing between them is the best course of action. She's a lovely distraction, but too much for the long run. A wound opens in my heart, and my ribs squeeze the empty cavity. She belongs here, while I….

"They may not want to listen, doll face, but I'm all ears." Teeth swaggers into Magda's space, wearing his predatory smile. He runs a finger down her cheek while letting her know he's looking down her dress. "What talents do you plan on bringing to our adventure? Do you cook? Wash dishes? Sew?"

"No, I—I—" she sputters in distress. Her fury melts into a familiar panic. "I've lived my life in three rooms. I'm a quick learner, but if it isn't in a book, I've never heard of it. Even what I read, I never practiced."

"No domestic skills? That's not a problem," he says with a playful tone. He flips his long blond hair over his shoulder and beams another smile at her. Wenches fall hand over fist for his act. There's no way to tell him to back off fragile Magda without claiming her as being under my protection, though. I don't want her under my protection, do I? "We've always got room for a doxie, haven't we, men?"

Over my dead body.

"What's a doxie?" Magda may be the same height as Teeth, but her innocence shrinks her to child-size. She crinkles her nose and squints her eyes at him in suspicion. He runs a hand down her back to rest on her bottom.

Someone snickers. I see red. *I'll gut him like a fish.*

"Well, beautiful, a doxie keeps the crew's spirits up…." He runs his fingertip just inside the neckline of her dress. "She uses her God-given assets to keep us in…fighting condition."

I shift my weight to the balls of my feet in order to pounce on the man—until the frost on her tone freezes me in place.

"I don't like to be called that."

"…but you are savvy to being a doxie, beautiful?"

"That's the second time you've called me *beautiful*. Now, you pay!" she hisses.

Her spindly arm grabs Teeth in a headlock. The shocked man falls like a split mast. She opens her mouth wide to display her fangs for all of us before biting down on Teeth's neck. His feet scrape at the muddy swamp, but he can't gain purchase. His fingers claw at her arm. His oblique position leaves him at her mercy as she slurps and gulps. No one comes to his rescue. If anything, the other men seem to have backed away a few steps.

To continue the adventure from the beginning with Magda, Branko, Chub, and Teeth read the Walk the Walk Paranormal Pirate series!

Walk the Walk

Book 5: Hooking Captain Teeth

Walk the Walk

Book 5: Hooking Captain Teeth

More Monster Brides Titles

Want to discover more beastly brides and monstrous grooms? Keep reading the Monster Brides Romance Series!

Haunted Hearts by S.C. Principale
Ripples For Skies by Teshelle Combs
Betrothed to the Yeti by Marilyn Barr
As the Tide Turns by Grace Mirchandani
The Vishap's Bride by Roslyn St. Clair
Claiming the Fae Crown by Lilliana Rose
A Wolf's Bargain by Rachel Abernathy
Venom Kissed by Sydney Winward
To Marry A Succubus by Roslyn St. Clair
Fated to the Tarasque by Roslyn St. Clair
Phoenix's Eternal Flame by Sofia Aves
Nothing to Hyde by S.C. Principale
'Til Death Do Us Part...Or Not by Annee Jones
In Love with the Leshy by Danielle Sibarium
Marrying My Moth Lady by Marilyn Barr
The Vampire's Mistress by D A Nelson
Bite Me Tender, Bite Me Sweet by V.V. Strange
Kraken's Vow by Raven Hush
His Undercover Wolf by Susan Horsnell
Tide to the Selkie by Serafina Jax
Hooking Captain Teeth by Marilyn Barr
Stone Cold Groom by S.C. Principale
Bonded to the Boo Hag by Mikayla Rand
The Rusalka and Mr. Right by S.C. Principale
Bigfoot Finds A Bride by Jenny Fenshaw

Walk the Walk

Book 5: Hooking Captain Teeth

About the Author

Marilyn Barr lives in the wilds of Kentucky with her husband, son, and rescue cats. She has nine books with The Wild Rose Press in multiple romance subgenres from sweet, new adult romance to erotic, fantasy romance. She loves to place monstrous characters with hearts of gold in historical romances and her historical, paranormal romances have won the Crowned Heart Award, 2nd place in National Excellence in Story Telling (NEST) Contest, Imadjinn Award for Best Paranormal Romance, and Grand Finalist for the InD'Tale Magazine's RONE Award.

When engaging in the real world, you can find her with the Kentuckiana Romance Writers, volunteering with her son's Special Olympics teams, or dancing around her kitchen. She is a sucker (haha) for cheesy horror movies, Italian food, punk music, black cats, bad puns, and all things witchy.

Connect with her on social media to witness her writing journey, shelter cats' shenanigans, steamy book reviews, and hilarious witch fails.

More Books by Marilyn Barr

Snuggling Under Snowdrifts

Cuddling My Chuchunya
Spooning My Chuchunya
Cherishing My Chuchunya
Embracing My Chuchunya
Forgiving My Chuchunya (coming in 2025)
Holding My Chuchunya (coming in 2025)

Walk the Walk: Vampire Pirate Romance

Walk the Plank
Walk the Deck
Walk the Night
Quartermaster (Part of the Mortar & Pestle Series)
Hooking Captain Teeth (Part of the Monster Brides Series)
Shiver Me Satyr (Part of the Time for Monsters Series)

Monster Brides (Multiauthor Series)

Betrothed to the Yeti
Marrying My Moth Lady

Walk the Walk

Book 5: Hooking Captain Teeth

Tied to Ms Krampus (coming in 2024)

Monstrous Standalones

Hell of a Husband (Free on Marilyn's Website)
Clutching Cthulhu's Pearls (Coming in 2025)

Strawberry Shifters

Book 1: Bear with Me
Book 2: Round of Applause
Book 3: Go Scorch Yourself
Novella 3.5: Smoother Than Spumoni
Book 4: Rotten Apple
The 5th Wheel (In the Beyond the Veil Anthology)

KRW Charity Anthologies

Ace of Diamonds (Part of Double Down on Love)

The Spiritual Spy

The Spy Who Was Out Cold (Free on Marilyn's Website!)
The Spy Who Loved My Russian Tea Cakes

Printed in Dunstable, United Kingdom